BOTH
WAYS
HOME

Poems
and
Stories

James H Duncan

Alpine Ghost Press

ISBN   979-8-218-08033-4 (paperback)

Credits:
"Strange Gods of the Prairie" appeared in *The Gasconade Review*
"Sanctuary" appeared in *San Antonio Review*
"Saint Michael" appeared in *Book of Matches*
"A Splinter" appeared in *Trampoline*
"Picturesque" appeared in *Vita Brevis Press*
"Riverwalk" appeared in *The Rye Whiskey Review*
"even the immortals know" appeared in *Front Porch Review*
"Death & Co." appeared in *Cajun Mutt Press*
"Both Ways Home" appeared in *San Pedro River Review*
"Patroon Island Bridge" appeared in *Trailer Park Quarterly*
"May the Moon Shine On" and "Wednesday Sunset South Main Ave." appeared in *Roadside Raven Review*
"Transience" and "Driver Dave" appeared in *Dumpster Fire Press*
"Ode to Madison Avenue at 6:15 p.m." and "Topo-Chico" appeared in *Day Job Journal*
A version of "The dead release their names to me" appeared in Lantern Lit, Vol. 1 under the title "Theft"
A version of "Little Victory Diner" appeared in the book *Nights Without Rain*

Thank you to Amy Kefauver for her feedback on the stories within.

This book is for **Amelia**, who has made coming home the best thing I ever did, and for **Jesse**, who I haven't seen in years but who I visit every time I sit down to write.

1

Author's Note

One could argue that I haven't gotten very far in life, considering I live less than a mile from the hospital where I was born in Albany, NY. On the other hand, I feel extremely lucky to have seen as much of this country as I have, navigating highways from one coast to the other and crossing the Mississippi like stitching a wound. But no matter where I went or where I lived, I eventually ended up in one of my two hometowns: Albany and San Antonio, TX. Albany is where my mother's family is from, San Antonio is where my father's is from, and I've spent huge chunks of my life in both places. But when I was in one place, I was thinking of the other, and when I lived in neither I thought about both, always wishing I could spend more time with family and friends so far away. But you can't be in two places at once, and time doesn't stop no matter how much you ask it to, so I always felt like I was missing out, far from home, even when I was sitting at home. But having two hometowns is also a blessing. I revel in the memories of the people I've known in both places who made those cities special. If we ever shared a drink, shared a laugh, shared a holiday, shared a job, shared a roof, or shared a family, you meant something to me, and you made those places, those two hometowns, indelible in ways that even a whole book of poems and stories cannot properly express. But I tried here, and I hope you enjoy. Thank you.

James H Duncan

June 20, 2022
Albany, NY

I have seen both sides
of this highway

home my eternal mirage

dawn in the rearview,
  the setting sun
          inevitable

ALBANY,
NEW YORK

Albany

of my city the worst I've ever said was:
you are the grayest city in America
and you are where fun goes to die;
stranger after stranger would smirk
and nod at my terrible jokes of home
and yet they knew nothing of you,
I knew nothing of you having left
so young and spent so long taking
and acquiring and stealing and cataloging
memories and knowledge and mileage
and now I see with eyes renewed the
green foliage billowing along the Hudson
as blue tarpaulin skies range along the
distant hills, the floodplains and tumbling
kills named by Dutch tongues and indigenous
translations, spawning colonies and crafters,
pillars and plowshares, steelworks and
highways, bridges and theaters, thinkers
and grifters, children and yard bulls,
deadlines and desolation, empty homes and
barren fields, tall grass and shorn hearts,
raised fists and rainbow crosswalks,
long nights and the faintest hints
of dawns yet to rise, but striving and yearning
and I knew nothing of such inspirations,
such visions, such Saturday nights
and cemetery Wednesdays
and the long avenues of reckless rain
that connect them, and nowadays
I might find myself with a book of Carl
Sandburg beneath a tree in Washington
Park and think, with dust on my shoes from
one coast or another, that I have arrived
full circle, and this city with all its

joy and loss and lapping waves and
neon Palace nights will be the end
of me, the last yellow leaf falling from
its final perch in the late October wind,
reaching the ground, skittering, settling
into the earth, so time and snow and
age beyond age may take me wherever
this spinning globe is heading next

Ode to Madison Avenue at 6:15 pm

the rich hue of lamppost light
daubing the nighttime sky
with neon honey and saffron, a dome
of incandescence revealing cracked sidewalks
and small dandelions reaching
up toward the moon, blooming under
the electric orange of humanity's humming addiction,
Edison's curse and gift, our soul in filament dosage
forming the sharp golden point of anticipation
for a night that is, as of yet, still too far away
for neon to make real

yet we wait, pulse with hope, and ebb along
the eastbound sidewalk in step with the moon
now caught in pine horizons and the rich
hue of lamppost light, we wait
we wait and pulse
with hope

Cul-de-Sac

voices carry from one yard to the next,
paper lanterns strung along
the scent of chlorophyll and bbq,
warm rubber hoses,
the evening dew

women in white jeans scolding
then kissing
the lips of ugly children

red-faced husbands screaming at televisions
and drinking domestic beer

amid the glow of domesticity
flickering against the orange-fire sunset
beyond the pool and treeline,
magnetized eyes drift away from
the blood pooling around the bodies
of Black children eleven miles away
as a police officer stands idly by
calling for a second ambulance
so he can go home to Family Feud
and pot roast

as eleven miles away the crickets
orchestrate the evening dim just
outside the sliding glass door

you sip the domestic beer they
give you, you eat the bbq chicken

you know it will all fall away

and in truth, it should

in truth, it's all an illusion
concealing the gears grinding
the have-nots into dust

in truth, this is one long commercial
distracting you until the power goes out

while elsewhere there is nothing
but static and sirens and
someone crying in the night

as crickets orchestrate
the soft eternity
just outside the sliding glass door

Picturesque

the place where you go to stare across the church yard
through pine trees and a chain-link fence to see
the apartment where you used to live, now unoccupied,
the landlord letting the place go, and you wonder
what became of it all, the front porch evenings, the
church bells that woke you all on Sunday morning to
talk of the night before then slipping back
into peaceful weekend naps,
the pipes that rattled all winter long, white
curtains billowing in the summer air,
and the knife you kept
on your nightstand in case the neighbor
became unreasonable again,
the sunflowers you planted along Morris Street
and the tomatoes you grew,
spiderweb cracks in every ceiling and every wall,
a world now hollowed out, swept up, boxed away,
walked through with the landlord, a deposit check
handed back, windows shuttered, electricity
turned off, no sign out front,
funerals we never attended, a cold wind sweeping
across church parking lots, lampposts illuminating a
life that doesn't exist anymore

and maybe never did

Upstate Autumnal

that seasonal magic of wildfire
and rose-gold devilry
blankets each sidewalk and street with
yellows and reds and daydreams of
skeleton corn fields rattling in that gentle
October Country in our mind
where the afternoon Sunday light lingers
before falling to richer, deeper, tapering midnights

let us run down these sidewalks to that place
of yesterday and behold
the falling orb of rust and glow,
carnival lights wavering toward the horizon,
jack-o-lantern heat smiling the distance of night,
succumbing to a last rictus grin
of overpowering joy and laughter, laughter,
I want to see you there, laughing
forever, long after
our bones
turn russet red to dust

and if you lie there long enough through eons and age
there will be a whisper coming from the treeline
calling you to rise up at last for the long journey
back to infinite sidewalks of shadows and
rose-gold devilry, all the way home at last

Bring Your Son

She worked for the state in Albany's capital plaza. Not the Corning Tower that dominated the skyline, but in one of the four smaller skyscrapers set in a line just behind it. From the ninth floor she could see the entire plaza: the boxy state museum and library on one end, the long reflective pool stretching hundreds of feet, and on the other end the capitol building, the state court offices, and The Egg, a theater space named after its shape—an egg with the top half sliced off. But it always reminded her of a failed spaceship, something that could take her elsewhere, anywhere, but wouldn't.

She didn't like Albany or the highways to get there, especially not the dark underground parking garage that always felt so damp and loud with the echoes of the highway nearby reverberating along the concrete levels and corridors. But she felt better once she made it inside walking the long marble esplanade, brightly lit white walls offset by colorful geometric murals and oversized impressionist sculptures. From there she took the grey elevator to her grey floor to her grey cubicle for another day of clerical filing, form verification, typing, copying documents for distribution, more typing, more filing, more mail runs, endless.

The letter from school asked parents to participate in "Bring Your Child To Work Day" if they were able, and he'd been so good. Not the best, but better than usual. He'd been sleeping in his own bed. He poured his own cereal *and* milk these days, without spilling. He bathed without complaint. But he still daydreamed too much at school and had wet himself three times in one month. Near misses, he said. He kept almost making it. She chalked it up to an unwillingness to interrupt, a shyness, but the teachers asked about his father, how often they saw one another, how life had been since the divorce. They thought he was stealing (and later found out he wasn't) and they talked about therapy when he cried at the holiday party. She didn't see the need, but she worried.

So she took him to work. He was small for his age and blond, but it was fading to brown now that he was six, just as her own hair had done when she was in kindergarten in Nevada all those years ago. He thrilled at the towers, the twisting highway offramps, the dungeon-like parking garage, and the expansive underground promenade full of art and hallways leading to all the various buildings that made up the plaza, as well as the food court inside where, to his excitement, they had both pizza and a McDonalds. But despite the glimmer of delight in his eyes as they wound through the marble halls and climbed aboard the elevator, he spoke quietly and stood close to her, his hand in hers.

He marveled at the view from her window and the height of her office, though it wasn't her office, just a room she shared with four others in open cubicles, but only one co-worker was in that day. She left him for a moment to find better coffee than the sludge in the break room. Alone now, he edged to the window again and looked at the cityscape below. He called it a canyon in his small mousy voice.

She appeared to his right and almost corrected him to say it was a plaza, but looking out beside him, a better word came to mind—plateau. The plaza rose out of the ground as a giant rectangle and within it all the boxy, modernist buildings rose in precise angles and distances from one another. It was as far from the dry, golden west as one could imagine. Instead of an arid landscape of canyon and plateau, Albany was but a damp and gray slate monument to bureaucracy.

Together they made copies at the big Xerox machine. He liked the smell of the warm paper. He helped her place red tabs on the pages where other people needed to sign them. Then he sat and read his book, *Charlotte's Web*, and when she looked up at him reading intently and swinging his legs in his chair, he looked just as he had in that doctor's office before the psychologist with gray hair in a ponytail and bifocals led him into her office. She waited impatiently, worried somehow that a shard of her divorce had lodged itself into her son's mind and that she'd never really find it until the damage was done. When the hour was over, the doctor came out and smiled at her.

"Your son is fine."

"They said he was too sensitive. And too quiet."

"He is sensitive and emotional but that's normal—he's six. Being quiet, reserved, that's one of the many ways in which children cope with changes and growth. Some feel things deeper, faster, and for longer, and they express it differently, maybe all at once and maybe in subtle drips and drabs. If he was violent, hitting other children, angry, then I would worry. But him? Don't worry."

"What should I do?"

"Bring your son back," she said. "We can focus on self-expression techniques and ways to tell people how we feel that are productive, creative, and maybe more direct. Teachers like direct. They have enough kids to deal with at once. They don't have a lot of time to unravel mysteries. Bring your son, and we'll work on that."

"But he's okay?"

"More than okay."

"What's that building down there," her son asked, pointing through her office window across the city. "It looks like a castle."

"Maybe it is," she said, smiling and watching him closely.

He looked around her office, the overhead lights glowing dull and steady, the gray-green carpet stained with years of foot traffic. He said, "Why can't you work there instead?"

"Well, I have to work where they tell me to work."

He considered that for a while, eyeing the empty desks all around him, and just when she thought he was going to go back to his book, he asked, "Will I have to work here too?"

She said no, not if he didn't want to. He'd work somewhere else, doing something wonderful and exciting and he'd enjoy himself. He'd be happy. She told herself that he'd be happy.

He glanced at her before sitting down and opening his book again. She looked at the papers on her desk waiting for her to file them, then at her son, wondering if happiness was something you found, or if it found you. A door shut somewhere. The boy read his book, and she watched him. The second hand of the wall clock spun in silence, and outside clouds blotted out the sun with indolent steel and the gentle suggestion of rain.

Patroon Island Bridge

my father once worked on this bridge
and warned of inevitability,
Swiss-cheese construction with
American intuition sealed into every
I-beam and misplaced bolt,
bubble gum and spit

it'll hold, they told him, for generations

they named it after an island that no
longer exists, the Hudson River reshaped
by time, by nature, by backfill to expand
the human footprint for shipping, for
riverside expansion, for a deeper graveyard
for PCPs, toxins, sludge, and bones

they built this bridge long after my great-
grandfather jumped into the Hudson
after losing his wife to disease, his children
to an orphanage, his job and soul and hope
to the American meat-grinder, and
they found him somewhere near Athens
along the riverbank, never witnessing
the construction of greater, taller bridges
spanning the murky gray expanse
that divides where he was born on one side
and where I was born on the other, a wound
that time can only make worse

I used to dream of crossing the Patroon Island
Bridge as a child, and in the dream I'd be three
or four and I'd always wake up in the back
seat of my mother's yellow station wagon
wearing my underwear and a white shirt

and no one behind the wheel of the car;
I was alone, and as the station wagon veered
toward the edge of the bridge, I'd crawl
into the front seat to grab the wheel but
the car crashes into the guardrail
and we fall, the car and I, toward that water

and then I wake up

I think of that dream every
time I cross the Patroon Island Bridge

but

I don't have dreams like that now, and
they won't find me near Athens or Catskill
or Poughkeepsie because I went through all
that and I'm still here, by luck or fate,
and so is the bridge, intuition and bubble gum
holding the steel and concrete erect as I pass
along its lanes heading east/west over and over,
testing my luck and testing my fate, testing the
American meat-grinder made stronger with
each passing generation until one day I too
am caught in the wheels and the teeth

but

they won't find me near Athens or Catskill

histories will repeat themselves,
and some sadnesses are buried as deep
as Hudson toxins, but I like my chances,
so long as I keep moving forward,
my heart beating me onward
toward home

Beating Golden Heart

in the quiet depths of night,
these streets and sidewalks transform
from broken concrete and asphalt
into star maps, pinpoints in time
with infinite space between the front lawn
and the end of the block where
Madison Avenue meets the silent
solar system of my life

and if you turn right at Andromeda
you will see a long neon-lit
alley of bars and cafes, and at the far
end is the glow of the theater, the marquee
a dazzling comet of red and flashing blue,
the big white board beneath announcing
silver halide wonders held in space and time:
Casablanca, Jaws, The Night
Of the Living Dead, Little Women, It's
A Wonderful Life, Rear Window, the bright lights
Cast from deepest darkness, pillars of white
crisscrossing the sky, announcing fate and desperate
adventure, love and our collective fall, all remarkably
visible from the corner of my block

even from the darkened driveways
and furthest reaches of my neighborhood
where I look up on other late-night walks and
see those stars in the sky, I know that the theater
is there, somewhere, beyond the tangle and thorns
of our small city wilderness and residential slumber,
a screen and a seat among the stars and the heavy pull
of celestial awe, a place to turn to when the edge
of the galaxy becomes too remote, too dark,
as it feels tonight

I pause on the edge
of some distant midnight sidewalk,
hover over the lip of the curb, breathe,
and watch as the sparkling lights
of the marquee dazzle
along the streets into the shadows,
blinking, reflecting, gone,
like so many hours and days
of my life, but my life
is still here, still spinning and flashing
with more features coming soon,
so I spin this tin can body
180 degrees and
head back toward that cinematic marvel,
no matter the distance, no matter
the cold or the hunger of the void

my controls always set
for the center of that great
beating golden heart
of this small rock I call home

Love, Wild

can you fathom the meaning of love?
snapping bottle-rockets in the sun
    coming from all directions,
sit in the cemetery grass mowed and bristled
    as all the other families
arrive by the carload, Albany
across the river to the west, and can
you feel the weight of anticipation in
the air? isn't that love? isn't it?

broad oak canopies like green thunderheads
shade stone and minivans alike,
children squirming in the laps of mothers
    as fathers swat away black flies,
almost time, almost here, the horizon
scarlet melding purple breathing black
    almost here, almost time, the war of
the worlds in one fire-punch exposition

and there they go!

reflective dazzlement in the eyes of toddlers
crowding around, their heartbeats radiant
in the warm tide of summer nights,
    endless screams in public pools, ice
cream trucks prowling their delights
    before turning September's corner into
rolling hills of green and yellow, yellow
and orange, orange and red, red and brown,
    brown glowing wild in reflective jack-
o-lantern light flickering from every stoop
and window throughout Pine Hills,
Buckingham Lake, Green Island,
    the steep ascents throughout Arbor Hill,

Center Square and Sheridan Hollow,
Rensselaer, Castleton, Delmar's four corners,
hunkered homes bracing against autumn
winds snapping their teeth, baring
    winter claws white and sharp and then it
comes: the bluster and wild snows from
    Great Lakes beyond, and we fortify our
souls with lights and candles and pine and love,
ages passing from one year to the next,
the weight of life piling deep, too deep to
    shovel out, too cold and too steep and too
late the rising sun—the sun rising, melting
the bite, thawing to gutters of slush and
somehow the bare arms and bones of the trees
    know it, they show it, budding into days
bright and blue and even the rain feels
fresh and breathless in the joy of another
winter behind us, the grass growing
    thick and heady, the elms, maples, tulips
in Washington Park blooming in tune
with the great turning clock hands unseen
until the explosions in the sky circulate
and spin, rain down like cascading palm trees
or double-helix hearts, the pop and crackle
excitations reflecting in the eyes of toddlers
crowding around the lawn chairs, straining
    to see, squirming in their mothers' laps
as fathers swat black flies before
the long walk home, the traffic, the beds
waiting for sleepy heads, can you feel it?
is that love? is it?

            if it isn't, it's something close

close enough to make
            this great journey worth it

you in your black jacket on Lark

coffee is one thing, but I knew it
when we walked from one end
of Lark Street to the other, the
winter wind blowing your black
hair, the way the snow danced
in their ephemeral strands,
the way your cheeks blushed
pink in the winter bite and the way
your eyelashes caught flurry white
flakes in a sideways glance
in the dim glow of passing
lampposts, and I knew
it, I knew it, I knew it
and I kept it inside for so long
afterward but all it took was
walking one end of Lark Street
to the other shoulder to shoulder
with you in the first snowfall
of November for my heart to
shudder and fall right into place

I, Stranger

I left the wedding early and stood beneath an awning outside the banquet hall on the edge of town. Schenectady was still considered a General Electric city, but only barely, as most of the behemoth factories had long ago closed, their distant lights sparkling through the mist and rain. I leaned against a brick wall and stared down at wet cigarettes in the dirt and questioned whether I should drive or wait, having had a handful of bourbon mixers. But the wedding was a sour affair, a cousin long estranged and the invitation came of familial necessity to balance out their roster. Stuck at a back table among the others who didn't fit in anywhere, I waited until they went to slice the cake with great fanfare and slipped out the back. No open bar. No welcome faces. The nighttime rain at the windows calling my name.

It felt good behind the wheel, smooth and insulated, far from forced chatter and loud dance music. I listened to the rain peck the windshield and the tires slicing through pools of water along the curb. I moved slowly through the older part of town, catching every red light and contemplating the neon signs of the liquor stores from the 60s, cockroach motels, dirty pizza parlors, empty laundromats, each one a relic from a time that wasn't any better than this, it just felt that way when you looked back at all we lost. But too many decades had passed by, too many folks moved out, too few with decent jobs remained, and the weeds grew like wildfire after the springtime rain.

I played Tom Waits as I put the lights of town behind me, passing long stretches of wooded lots and vacant strip malls heading east. Somewhere ahead I'd find Albany in no better shape, especially not this late at night. "Drunk on the Moon" softened the windshield wipers to a gentle refrain, back and forth as they whispered the rain away, sometimes with a squelch as the last of the rain dissipated to a fine mist. I didn't want to go home but I didn't want to drink in some random bar surrounded by strangers who'd only made me feel lonelier. I wanted to park somewhere and listen to the night as Tom Waits hummed through the speakers, barely audible, a somber friend telling me tales and fabrications, dreams and soliloquies.

I always enjoyed driving around Albany at night, weaving the highway interchanges from 87 to 90 to 787, taking a random exit, cruising the somnolent neighborhoods, the subdued shopping centers after closing time, encountering the pockets of nightlife here and there. Albany doesn't have a dedicated downtown where you congregate and remain. The bars are scattered like outposts in the night. Lark Street, Pearl Street, Broadway, Madison, up 787 to Troy's resurgent downtown, a honeycomb of taverns and cocktail lounges, oyster bars and dives. Or you venture into the bedroom communities and find the one neon Coors sign in a window, the parking lot full of old pickups, the crickets orchestrating the melancholy of time passing relentless.

Not long before the wedding invitation came, I made myself a mix CD (which ages me to a very particular generation of geriatric millennial) consisting of Miles Davis tracks mixed with Jack Kerouac and Charles Bukowski reading their poetry. I put it in somewhere along my cruise down I-90 passing the exits for 787 toward downtown Albany, and Jack began speaking of the Subterraneans as I crossed the Hudson. The gulf of dark forests on the other shore swallowed me as I drove further east, into the realm of my youth.

I took the Miller Road exit on a whim and cut through the silent, dark stretch of back country roads where I grew up. I passed the hillside where I picked wild raspberries as a child. I passed the house where two teenagers killed their stepmother with a hammer in the early 90s, and every time we drove by that house my mother would say, "That poor man lost his whole family in one day."

I drove by my childhood dentist, then the Brown Derby, and even the old Thruway Beverage, a small warehouse-looking purveyor of beer and wine that hadn't changed one rusty iota since before I was born. And finally, I saw the sign for Green Meadow Elementary School, where I attended grades K through 4 in the last half of the 1980s. I drove down the side road, passing the dark parking lot, and pulled off at the gravel side of the road overlooking the playground and fields behind the school.

In 1990, my father drove three days from Texas to watch my sister and I play in this playground. He'd park his small red pickup truck a few spots to the right, near the small tree that now towered over the gravel pull-off. We loved that truck and the small assortment of cassette tapes he brought along on his trip: Tom Petty, Traveling Wilburys, U2, Van Halen, Stevie Ray Vaughn. I like to think that if he and I were the same age in 1990, we would have been friends. But as it was, I was only his son, a 10-year-old boy who loved his father's music and the way he'd spin us on the metal merry-go-round before driving us to the mall for food and a movie as George Harrison sang "Handle With Care" through the truck speakers.

I got out of my car and stood in the light rain, under low roiling clouds barely lit by the scattered porch lights nearby. Across the field, the playground looked like a series of humps in the dark. I hadn't seen the school in years and I realized, even in the darkness of the overcast sky, that they replaced the massive old wooden playground with a much smaller one made of plastic, the metal slides, monkey-bars, and swings also pulled up and replaced. I walked out there. The tall grass wicked at my ankles, my toes getting damp in my sneakers, and I stood amidst the red and yellow plastic infrastructure.

I felt unlike myself in that moment. Like my muscle memories were gone and I had to operate on manual intention, working a mechanism of bone and flesh to turn and blink and try to understand how this space detached itself from my timeline to become something so foreign and strange, so small, so ethereal in the night. Were these rounded loops and towers a plastic ship from an extraterrestrial explorer, or was I the stranger? Some traveler from another time and place standing in the rain on an otherwise perfectly normal playground in suburban America? Who didn't belong here? Me, or it?

When I got in the car Miles Davis was just finishing "Round Midnight," so I started the song again and backed out of the gravel pull-off. I didn't want to go home but I couldn't stay here.

I drove into the night and tried not to think too much about how quickly the years had ticked by since 1990, since kindergarten, since my father was a child, since Jack Kerouac leaned forward and spoke into a microphone in a booth somewhere far from Albany and its tangled knot of highways. Instead, I headed for the onramp to I-90 westbound and closed my eyes as I accelerated, listening to the rain, the wheels on the blacktop humming louder and louder, and the deep inhale coming from the speakers before I opened my eyes to the next great improvisation.

Hypnosis

in the back seat of my grandfather's car, I listen
as The Shadow in all his old-time radio glory
remains out of sight as he stalks crime, his laughter
cutting through the night, headlights showing a parking
lot coated with snow, wood fencing, a road, and my
grandfather speaking to another man for a very long
time as the car idles and keeps me warm and I sit and
listen as my cassette plays the laughter of The Shadow,
the bitter fruit of crime withering on the vine,
and when the cassette turns to static I close my eyes
and wait for my grandfather, wait for time to come
and spin the hands of the clock in my heart
and abandon me to the cold of the future, alone
to fight the evils of mankind until I too
hear the laughter in the dark
and envision the lonely snowfall of my final
warm night on this earth

Somnolence

the shade of blue in your
mother's room made bright
by the streetlight ebbing through her
age-old curtains,
parted just enough
for a strip of white to cross her bed,
a mattress firm but giving

you lie there as a house-sitting son
on a weekend when you
should be out finding a future among the small
town bars and gatherings, but instead
there is a dog downstairs,
a book, the clothes dryer humming

and the blue light of your mother's room,
standing in the hallway looking in,
missing the mother of your youth as well
as the mother you know you
will lose one day, and you
hope this room holds her
world still and complete for just a little while longer

or as long as the gods allow

the dead release their names to me

the dead release their names to me
full, middle, and last
carved into stone, written in
black ink onto newsprint gray
pages across the Sunday morning table

sometimes it's the only gift they have left,
offerings we don't hear, the unbound
vocabulary clinging to this world while
everything else has moved on, the dreams and
habits and colloquialisms and souls
drifting through the higher branches
of the oak trees lining Oakwood Avenue,
then further into time, space unending

Otis Jefferson Portsmouthe
Phillip Maynard
Patricia Oddsman
Aaron Andernoch
Beverly L Lynnwood

but you were more than just a name,
more than recycled newsprint,
more than moss-covered stone, a hyphen
between two years beneath the shade
of maples turning green to red to brown
in the Hudson Valley autumntime

I accept your gift, not forgotten, but
revived, perhaps even revitalized, pardoned
from the void and sewn into the fortunes of another
soul,
into new pages that might turn in someone
else's hand so that someone might sing

your song tonight, every night,
the notes held aloft and hailed,
saviors of the living and the dead

Home

does one lungful of air recognize
that the other exists?
                do arteries
and veins communicate in the hush
between heartbeats?
                is the moss
growing on the north side of the roof
aware of the tufts of unmowed
Kentucky bluegrass basking along the
southern hillside of home?

home; the privilege of
singularity

my left hand and right hand
know very well
what the other is doing, holding
the steering wheel at 10 and 2 as
miles pass by, each one bringing me
closer to the other half of my marrow

I close my left eye and see
the world askew; I close my
right eye and see the world
askew; I close both and feel
the highway pull me toward
a certain fate I am not ready
to embrace, and so…

I live with both eyes open in a place
where two halves
   can never make a whole,
where the horizon always
whispers a promise it can

never keep,
where the two hands of the
clock spin opposite one another,
                              time
running out and adding up
at the same pace, making the weight
of everything I've missed over
                        the years
crush my fleeting moments in the now
with the nostalgic regret of impossibilities

I don't know what it is like
to be home
knowing there is no other home
waiting for me beyond the walls
and fences
and treelines and highways and lines
on a map marking territory and plates
tectonic and gravitational pulls
and the fringes
of the known galactic universe

home; the privilege of being
of knowing
of resting at long last in the pattering
whisper of summer rain on the back porch at night

home; divide me, but we
will be one
when the hands of the clock pause at north
by southwest
where my final sun will set
at long last

Deluge

the ravine is forged by frigid water,
rocks wet and sharp, so place your feet
carefully and work your way down
through the years, past heartbreak and desire,
past wonderment and imagination,
past blinking eyes dawning on a new world,
a primitive Hudson Valley without
a single prayer spoken or heard,
be in that place, crawl along that precipice,
and see if the trees are still there,
green and damp in the yawning dawn of sky,
the heartbeat forest, the forever horizon
blanked out by mist, hiding every moment
you forgot to love and keep dear,
safe from the damp, the dew pooling,
trickling back toward the cycle
of beginnings and endings, forged
of frigid waters in the yawning dawn of sky
and when you are ready, it will
accept you with a frigid embrace, heartbreak
and desire, wonderment and a horizon
blanked out by mist out there beyond one
final precipice leap into forever

Twelve-Gauge Shotgun

I didn't much care for hunting. It surrounded my
world, but it wasn't my world, or at least I didn't want
it to be when I was a young teenager, barely a teenager.
The timeline is fuzzy to me now, but I recall myself at
thirteen or so and feeing like the weight of the twelve-
gauge shotgun might tip me over if my balance shifted
too far this way or that. It was a beast of a weapon
compared to the only other one I'd fired, a small .22
rifle we used to shoot Coke cans and soda bottles in a
remote farm field under the vague supervision of
nearby parents who were more attentive to sighting
their own deer rifles with intricate scopes and long
leather straps. The .22 was a toy by comparison, but
later that year our fathers wanted us to hunt rabbits,
and rabbits meant shotguns.

    Rabbit hunting is a long and laborious chore of a
day. They usually took us to a vast rumpled field full
of boulders, scrub brush, scraggly trees, and swampy
wetlands full of cattails just east of Route 9 in Latham,
where you could see the road and the backsides of
businesses in the distance. It never felt remote enough
to me for firing guns, but the others fired theirs often
when we would drive through the brush to scare out
the cottontails from their winter hideaways. The smell
of frozen dirt and wet wood mixed with the smell of
exhaust drifting from the distant roadways. The snow
came knee high in most places. The frigid wind
barreled across the open fields. Yet sweat rolled down
my back beneath the many layers of thermals and puffy
overalls that made us move like the Stay Puft
Marshmallow Man from *Ghostbusters*, lumbering in
the snow, gun at the ready, watching for prey.

    But I never watched for prey. I'd look across the
icy fields illuminated by flat gray light above,

35

seemingly dusk at all hours, and at the twinkling halogens of the businesses and cars all along Route 9. I'd daydream about those cars, the warmth of their heaters, the freedom to go anywhere, a diner, a movie theater, somewhere warm down south, the occupants heading out on some great adventure in the west. Or I'd ignore the lights and imagine myself at war, stalking the winter forests of eastern France, guarding our exposed forward line during a lull in the shelling and chaos. Staring out across the desolation, I wondered when all this death and killing might end.

I daydreamed anytime they took me hunting anywhere, because I wasn't interested in killing. Did I eat the fruits of their labor, the work done by my uncles and stepfather and cousins? Yes. Venison and turkey and fowl and rabbit. Even the day long act of draining and skinning the animals, prying off their choicest parcels of muscle and organs for seasoning and freezing, was preferable to the immediate aftershocks of killing an animal. I'd killed half a dozen rabbits, no deer, no fowl, a small handful of fish, but nothing else. Firing the bulldozer of a shotgun and walking up to find the stricken rabbit bleeding out in the snow made me feel like, I don't know, like I broke a promise to someone, like I took what wasn't mine and the Lord (who I grew less and less interested in as my teenage years waned) stood above somewhere with disappointed eyes. I took what He gave and who was I to do so? A thirteen-year-old boy with a twelve-gauge shotgun.

One afternoon as we edged toward true dusk, a line of us, maybe three men and four boys, walked through the cattails, our last push to scare out the cottontails in the fields along Route 9. The snow was deeper in there, almost thigh deep in some places, and the tall reeds, all sickly golden and brown, obscured our view of each other. I only knew my cousin was somewhere thirty feet to my left through thick clusters of cattails. I trudged forward with heavy, rubbery steps, exhausted and disinterested, daydreaming, when a rabbit appeared.

The small brown creature leapt into view and stopped, twitching as it turned its black eyes upon me. I froze. It didn't move. We stared like that for five seconds, ten, fifteen, still it didn't move and I wondered why this animal presented itself to me so easily, so openly. I felt steam rising up from my wet hands, heated by the constant trudging, my insides boiling as I stood in the frozen tundra of cattails and reeds with this rabbit.

I lifted my shotgun and fired three feet to the rabbit's left. It bolted into the air and disappeared, the reeds shifting in the wind as I stared at the hole I made in the snow, nowhere near the animal's tracks. I felt relief at having driven away the animal with the devastating power of the twelve-gauge shotgun. I heard someone call out to ask if I bagged anything. I shouted no, and I could hear the others continue to trudge forward.

I turned and worked my way through the reeds and scrub brush to the line of trucks that stood in the parking lot of a closed banquet hall, the sounds of Route 9 now loud enough to mute the occasional popping of gunfire behind me.

Prying off my boots, my heavy puft overalls, I climbed into the truck cab, the twelve gauge beside me emptied of shells, the Ray Bradbury book I brought along for the drive waiting on the dash. But it was almost too dark to read and so I stared at the slate gray skies instead, waiting for the others, closing my eyes to sleep in my foxhole, the guns on the horizon silent, the battle over, the weary armies of tomorrow resting

while they could until the next push forward into
unknown horizons of doom.

Friday Morning Matador

for the first time in three weeks
I stepped outside and discovered
it was no longer freezing,
instead I found damp
sidewalks and slumped mounds
of dirty white snow,
a grayscale morning of cold fog
and springtime dampness as I walked
up the street to find coffee and eggs

about halfway up the block
a man walked into the street and began to
shout a name; he ran, stopping
and cutting in a new direction, and I saw
it was a loose dog, a great brown
shaggy thing that looked like some
sort of puffy toy that would supplant
a young couple's desire for children
but it outgrew this role and now it
was a monster that had run away
from home, no more cage or kennel,
no more leash or demands to lie
down to wait for a plastic cup
of dried food and a dirty bowl of water

now it was free, and the man
kept screaming, frantic, spinning and circling,
getting close but slipping in
the snow in his cheap sneakers
without any socks
as the dog evaded him
through the front yards up and down
the South Pine Ave, and soon the dog froze
across from me and looked my way and

it all stopped for a moment
—silence

the dog stared and I wondered: should I help?
should I kneel and pretend I had a scrap
of food to lure it over for this crazed man
in dirty sweatpants and winter jacket to
grab it and bring it home?

would I be the one to send it back to
the kennel, punished, a bad dog?
why me?
and so, selfishly perhaps, I decided not to
involve myself and the dog ran away again
as the man followed, shouting, crazed

I turned the corner and tried not to feel
guilty about not helping, and of course
in my state of guilt-struck overthinking
I walked through a pool of water that ran
icy cold over my ankle and soaked my sock

so, I limped the last fifty yards
to the coffee shop,
which was almost full,
one stool left at the counter

as I sat down, a busboy dropped a bin
full of dirty dishes across the floor—a child
began to cry and someone did that 'slow clapping'
like a real jerk

I ordered my coffee
and eggs and watched others
help the busboy
and I felt some relief at this

but also at the idea
that the man chasing the dog was not
the only one facing down the small tedious
tragedies of the day, an arena of charging bulls
swirling all around us, you and I and the busboy
and the man chasing the dog and the postal
carrier smoking outside the window weighed down
by bulky bags that never stopped coming, all
of us matadors with no capes or swords or
spears, each of us spinning on one dry foot
as fate tried again and again
to gore us, drive the horn deep into
our stomachs, but we keep moving, knowing
that final fatal blow and deafening applause
is somewhere out there, searching for us

they were out of half-and-half
that morning, too

Who Lives There?

"Who lives there?" people ask when they see it. The house on the corner. Something between Colonial Mansion and Tudor Cottage, and I see people stop at the corner and look up. I stand there with my coffee and look up, too. Everyone looks up. They don't see the intricate, painted-glass windows along the basement, or the rabbits who make burrows in the old rose bushes. They look up at the dark wood beams along the roof. They look up at the spires and the garrets. The ghosts in the windows. The old TV antennae on the roof. The slate tiles covered in moss. No one lives there, and it used to be an old day care center, but it's empty now and sometimes you see ghosts in there. I wasn't going to skip over that part. I just wanted to let it settle into place. Sometimes when it rains you need to let the pools of water settle until you can see the bottom with calm, pristine vision. Can you see the ghosts now? The top right window? Sometimes the top left. So what. Big deal. Every house is haunted a little. Sometimes only the dust bunnies know, but they're there. They don't usually see you or bother you because they think they're alive too, going about their business. But if they do see you, they think *you* are the sudden intrusion, the spectral wonderment of astro-planes beyond. We're all alive and living in these houses and sometimes we see each other and think, "What was that?" Then some people make TV shows about that, carry equipment and superstition into house after house, broadcast their pantomimes out across the seas and the mountains, zipping into countless TV antennae. But usually, we leave each other alone. They stare down at me with my coffee and think, "What is that man doing?" And I look up and think, "Ghost— upper left window." But it used to be a day care center for little kids. That must have been weird for everyone.

"What are all these kids doing here?" Then the kids went away, leaving it empty. Soon enough, however, someone will move into that house. There's a U-Haul truck pulling up outside just now, an orange and silver one with a big illustration of the Saint Louis Arch on the side, but the plates say New Jersey. I hope they like the stained-glass windows and the rabbits and the beautiful wrap-around porch that extends out into the yard, cantilevered beneath a towering pine tree. It's a beautiful house, the house on the corner. The one that makes people ask, "Who lives there?" We're all going to find out soon, I hope.

A Splinter

my used copy of *Harvest Poems 1910 - 1960*
by Carl Sandburg has the inscription: "purchased
in Connemara (Ireland) 1996 where goats-milk
fudge was being sold," and on page 82 there's
a newspaper clipping from The Fayetteville Times
about a ceremony in Flat Rock celebrating Carl's
body of work, a clipping yellowed by time and
the sun, held flat against a poem reading, "The
voice of the last cricket / across the first frost /
is one kind of good-bye / It is so thin a splinter
of singing"—a finer poem I have never written,
or read for that matter, and that is why I advise
you to never buy books new, for all the treasure
you might leave behind

Other Possibilities

the shadows here
on South Pine Avenue
grow too accustomed
to silence

the weeds outside
reach ever higher
while
I shiver down
closer
to the grave
with each passing day

who will tend this land
when I'm gone?
who will walk these halls
and flick the lights
on and off?
or close the window?
call your name?

outside there's a mail truck
idling at the corner,
I can see it there, waiting

things end

thing don't end

but for now
I will dust this bookshelf,
trace the sunlight on the wall,
whisper adorations
and minor conspiracies

to you or anyone
who will listen

as the weeds outside reach
ever higher

and the mail truck moves on
to other possibilities

The Road That Leads Home

if you follow the lines on the map
and navigate the sequence of dots
to a place you call home, you're just
as likely to find yourself in a town
you've never known, a bed you don't
understand, a fever dream you cannot
break out of, and it all has the same
name, it all has the same broken shell
when you hammer it open and play
with the yolk of the hours and meaning-
less excuses, but sometimes that map
folds in some strange back-pocket way
and you flatten it across the hood of
your car and scan the creases and stains
and look up and you see your four walls
alight with some new aura, a pulse
belonging to a different heart that always
existed just a block away, a mile away,
within the same sphere of the little
white dot on the road map you had used
for years and years, always ending up
in the same old place, until finally
it all changed; a streetlamp set some new
voice aglow within your heart, and you
let that map fall from your hands into
the gutter flooded with rain; you take
those steps up; you close the door behind
you for good, or so you hope, you dream

you wake

Poem for Pine Hills on a Tuesday Night

in soft amber dusk and blue haunted
alleys and yards, the end sidles closer
reaching through vines coiling around
fenceposts and the bubbling fountains
in back gardens, past silent screen doors
and shuttered windows holding back
the night, the coming stars, the moon
the somber ennui of youth unattainable

in soft purple dusk and shadow haunted
streets and porches, the end sighs out
along with gentle billows of western
wind and the rattle of still-green leaves
that will slowly yellow and brown and rust
themselves to death in a matter of weeks
revealing claws and limbs knotted that
aim to catch the moon and stars but won't

in soft onyx midnight and nightlight haunted
hallways and bathrooms the end curls up
within your bones and cells, burrowing its
home among your dreams and worries, your
vacation plans and children's lunch schedules,
your meditations and promises to your god

as you roll to the cool side of the pillow,
the end yawns in unison and dreams of dawn,
when every little thing will finally begin, at last

Overnight Security

I dyed my hair blond in the summer of 2000. I don't
remember why, but it wasn't why people said, that I
wanted to be like Eminem. Everyone called me Slim
Shady afterward anyway, but I don't remember
thinking about him when I did it. It just happened.

I was in Texas and had just finished the last class
of my freshman year when I stopped at HEB and
bought a bottle of hair dye, went home, and did it. I
think now that I just wanted to be someone else.
Anyone else. I didn't like who I was at that moment,
having failed too many easy classes at UIW, a college I
only applied to last minute because the Marines said
my vision was too bad for them to take me on the
summer before. I failed so many classes, in fact, that I
lost my scholarship and was academically suspended. I
worked too many night hours at a chef's job I didn't
like and I never studied, fell asleep in class, and
wandered aimless whenever I had breaks. I wanted to
be a playwright but it wasn't going well. I didn't know
theater. I didn't know how to write. I didn't know
anything. When it ended, I couldn't think of what came
next—so, out came the bottle blond.

I went back to campus just to walk around the
next day and no one recognized me, or maybe no one
said hello because I hadn't really made any friends, but
when I left campus I did feel a little better, a little more
anonymous despite the blast of neon yellow hair on my
head. Continuing the series of inexplicable decisions, I
left my '72 mustang behind with my dad, packed up
most of my belongings into two suitcases, and flew
home to upstate New York. I told myself I was just
visiting. I wasn't.

Things were no more welcoming or purposeful
back home, and I ended up sleeping most nights at my

friend Jesse's apartment in downtown Troy. We'd
drink cheap wine coolers in the summer heat while I
read on the couch and he watched Showtime with the
volume off, occasionally flipping through a graphic
novel. We shared sandwiches at Manory's diner, or
we'd each buy one and save half for our dinner later.
We scraped by, a ramshackle life, using old beer
bottles to drink tap water, using take-out utensils for as
long as we could because we didn't have cutlery. It
was the kind of place where you had to plunge the
shower drain to keep the water flowing. The kind of
place where the downstairs neighbor would skip his
meds and throw the garbage cans up the stairwell in
irrational fits of madness. We drank, we read, we
looked for jobs in the local newspapers.

I called Blockbuster twice but they never replied.
Maybe they saw I still owed money on rentals down in
Texas. I interviewed at Stewart's and Best Buy but
neither called me back. The woman at JC Penny
scolded me for not having printouts of my resume, a
white dress shirt, or a clean shave. She called my hair
ridiculous and said I arrived with "a loser's mentality."
I ate a plain donut on the way home and stopped to
watch the Hudson River flow south for a while and
thought about how my grandfather's father jumped
from a bridge in Albany the 1930s and washed up near
Athens a few days later.

Jesse found a job with a security agency that
required three days of training, all paid, and they'd take
almost anyone without a criminal record, so that meant
us. The instructors and fellow guards called him Tex-
Mex. They called me Slim Shady. Neither of us liked
this, but that's how it was. After three days of classes,
they gave us special ID cards and jackets that said
SECURITY on the back, with the company logo on the
chest and arm.

They posted us in the same building in downtown Albany, working the same overnight shift where we'd always work with a third veteran guard. The vets liked Jesse a lot more because he talked a lot more, and they'd send me to do the routine patrols on each floor of the skyscraper twice a night while they talked at the lobby's security desk. I'd walk the rows of offices or the empty floors undergoing renovations, swinging my flashlight into this corner or that room. Shadows darted and I heard knocks and whispers, but it was just in my mind. They joked that the place was haunted, and even if it was ghosts it didn't really matter. Someone had to walk the floors, so why not me?

Bert was the oldest guard, well into his sixties, and he didn't like either of us but he liked me least because of my hair, which was still yellow. It was growing out slowly but not fast enough. He told me to go raise the American flag on the pole out front one morning but I screwed it up so badly he stormed out and berated me in front of people coming into work for disrespecting his sacrifices to the country and all who died in the mud and shit in Vietnam. Jesse laughed on the drive home at 8 a.m. and I did too.

Jesse could adapt to any schedule, could work sixty, seventy, eighty hours a week, sleep through lunch, and do it all over again. He fell into the overnight schedule without a hitch. I couldn't sleep during the day to save my life. I'd fidget and read and watch TV all morning until afternoon came and then I'd sleep off and on until it was dark out. I'd wake, eat, and I'd want nothing more than to sleep again but I showered and put on my SECURITY jacket and climbed into my borrowed car to do it all again. For two months Jesse was the only human I spoke to because the other guards didn't give a damn and everyone else in my life was asleep when I was awake, and vice versa.

Then they moved us to a pair of smaller buildings next to each other over by the big arena downtown. We each worked with a veteran for a week and then we were alone each night. Jesse would come by to see me and I'd go to see him in the building next door, connected by a walkway. Sometimes he slept on the women's room couch on the 8th floor while I walked patrol. Sometimes I slept in the stuffed chair in the maintenance office in the basement while he walked patrol. Once I fell asleep on the couch in the lobby and woke at 7:15 a.m. to knocking on the glass doors. People arriving to work early. That didn't go over well.

I decided to use the time alone to write, hoping it might keep me up. Part of me held out hope that the playwright thing might still happen somehow. I outlined a play about a security guard slowly losing his mind who only heard from his friends and family through voicemails he'd play when he arrived home in the morning. Each message grew stranger and more desperate until it became clear he was already dead and all this was his hellish punishment for a life of sloth. I thought it was a good idea but I didn't have the skill or talent to get it quite right. I wrote it longhand on yellow sketch pads and I'd take smoke breaks in the back courtyard where metal picnic tables surrounded a water fountain.

I only started smoking to give myself something else to do, and one night I walked back to the courtyard, lighting up as I pushed through the back door, and I saw three men fighting, one against two, and the one had a knife. All three turned and looked at me as I froze and stared. Then the one with the knife lunged my way. I turned and caught the door right before it locked shut, which would have doomed me. I would have had to dig out my keys to reopen it, but I slipped in and slammed the door shut just as he hit it, his laughter and threats dulled by the glass and metal. I called the police but he was gone before they even picked up the phone.

Nothing came of it, but I quit smoking that night. It was only my second pack.

One week later Jesse worked a shift that I had off, and I agreed to go pick him up. When I got there, he said, "This shit's over. They caught me sleeping again and I've had it with working nights anyway."

"Well, what are we going to do? I really need the money."

He said he knew someone who could get us call center jobs at a bank, no cold calling, just fielding account questions and forwarding people on to the correct departments. We walked next door to the building where I usually worked overnights and we found Smitty, the guard who always relieved me when I worked. He wasn't our boss but we told him we quit. He was mad and said that's not how we're supposed to go about doing it, but we walked out and never answered their calls. We got our last checks in the mail, though, and when Jesse started at the call center I went over to the community college and registered for the fall, called my high school job at a local deli and asked to come back, and called my dad and said I was staying in New York, that UIW wasn't working out. He could keep the car or sell it. Whatever he wanted to do.

I knew it was a mistake to walk away from the college and the car and my dad, but I made it anyway. I don't know why I did. I wasn't following any logical plan or aiming to be this or that in the next stage of life. I guess I just wanted to keep trying something else until it all fell into place.

Autumn came and I still slept on Jesse's couch. The call center didn't work out and he was the assistant manager of a strip club in a seedy part of Troy by then. He got engaged to one of the dancers, a very kind woman with wonderful eyes from Texas who slowly shaped him into a human being. I worked the deli. I took classes. I tried. I did a little better, but only a little. Sometimes I'd stop by Jesse's for a cheap beer, talk about this and that just to feel human, and hug his fiancé goodbye on my way out.

Some nights I'd walk down by the river, watching the neon waver on the tide. I'd think of my great-grandfather and wonder how long can you wait for things to fall into place before you end up falling into the cold depths of a southbound river instead. Probably a while. A little while longer, at least.

Skyway

now the workers in hardhats are back
from their lunch and drilling away with
their pneumatic jackhammers as some
pick up this cone and move it here, pick
up that one and move it there, the long
trek into the Skyway, reshaping the old
highway onramp into a sweeping park
rising into the blue eastern sky and down
to the curb of the Hudson River with the
hope that accessibility might alter the
fate of such a misfortune, a city turning
its back on its greatest treasure, the
running ruined channels of the river
that now calls to us from its banks at
night when even the stars and moon
cannot reflect without pity and regret,
and so, the workers churn through the
blacktop and hew at steel with casual
grit to reshape the city one season at a time,
future Skyway debris dancing like dust
motes through the downtown avenues and
the side streets, the sounds of our collective
hope hammering away as children wait, as
food vendors wait, as older couples wait hand
in hand on their way to some movie house
or repertory theatrical, young couples off
to dinner and wild nights at pubs and taverns
lining the cobbled streets of Lark and Pearl
and avenues throughout overlooked Albany,
all of them waiting for that Skyway into the dawn
and all life's promises that lie in wait beyond

The Beasts of Eagle Street

all great beasts succumb to time, no matter their might
and their hunger, no matter their gilding and veneration

the two of you there, you are no different, both of you
dug in on Eagle St., gated and guarded, gun and god

you overlook this city, blind to the damage done,
dominating the skyline, hiding behind shadow and time

a great cathedral of brownstone and Christian shame
where pedophiles and abusers bathe in body and blood

a house of political power and bully-pulpit swagger
where governors grope and prowl, flex their fragility

two great banners snapping in the valley wind running
up the Hudson through broken homes and shelters

where the unhoused are left to rot and children roam
without hope, no beacon in the long dark night ahead

men in robes and suits stand behind their podiums with
words, words, words, words, words, words, words

to a man they fail us in the simplest, most bare-bone
realms of decency and honor, humility and ministration

to a man they have poisoned the wells, salted the earth,
ripped the beating hearts of innocence from children

to a man they have filled our eyes with anger and have
lowered our common good to decadent cruelty

political clawing and self-congratulations squirming

amongst pews and bishops in a grim gleeful ouroboros

a shameful display of power gone to kinetic waste
just gold and silk eaten in the faces of the starving

when I walk along Madison and make that turn onto
Eagle Street: behold, two creatures of civilization

I feel such shame, pity, and sadness for all the pain
that has leaked from such wretchedly failed institutions

tainting our discourse, our faith in one another, leaving
ruinous paths in the shadow of those beasts of Eagle St.

Ode to Two Rivers

it is true, there are
two rivers that run
through my life,
one wide and strong
and the other
narrow and shallow,
fading into a dried bed
of yellow stones
baking in the
radiant summer sun

the bridges that span
these two rivers could
not be more different,
one carrying cars
across gray concrete with
pillars rising from deep
below, broad and wide,
while the other bridges
are shaded by palms
and twisted oaks, arcs
of stone and wood for
pilgrims to walk from
one side to the other, a
matter of yards at most,
and at the apex one
can stand and look
down at flatbed boats
passing by with tourists
taking photographs or
pointing in the moonlight
as cantina lights dapple
the skin of the forever
blackened midnight water

I have crossed these bridges
so often there is no way to
count and I have sat beside
the idling flow of these
rivers throughout every
year of my existence, which
feels like only an instant
to my memory but more
like an eternity when I am
listening to the lapping,
watching the sun set,
hearing the music from
nearby cafes and boats,
and maybe I'm looking
into someone's eyes, and
maybe I am alone with
the moon and the tide,
either way, I know, when
the time comes, my ash
and bone will slip beneath
the tides of one, and then
the other, as a gift to the
two rivers for all they have
given me throughout the
years, the miles, the days,
and endless star-filled nights

at least that's my hope,
my wish, my dream carrying
me onward and out of sight

Midway

august love in the lights of the Tilt-a-Whirl,
endless tickets in hand,
the wide aisles smelling of sugar and deep fryers,
food truck aromas on the wind
rushing through Hudson Valley farmland carrying
the youthful cries of terror and ecstasy,
g-force romance and dazzling
blue neon, red neon, white,
immortality pinwheeling into the sky,
the rise and fall of stoic horses
grinning in the carnival lights, taking you
around and around and beyond,
love out of reach, love crashing home,
rotational contact, the moon
escaping into the treeline,
laughter, neon,
darkness, falling,
grasping the ticket all the way down
where her hair tangles into your
everlasting joyful cry for more

Topo-Chico

dancing in shards of green glass &
glinting along the wrinkled rhino
skin of the silent Sunoco gas station
somewhere west of Lake George,
I scry your fizzing carbonation in
afternoon sun like some ancient
village enchantress reading bones
and chicken blood, assaying futures
untenable, romances inadvisable, yet
teenage yearning knows no psychic
boundaries and seeks only visions
and indications through the scree of
debris and hormones, broken shards
of glass and Topo-Chico dissipating
into the heat of the afternoon as I
give up, return to the car, the beat-up
old VW Rabbit we have all taken east
on yet another aimless journey of the
heart toward nowhere, we return to
the highway, assailing and endless,
fever-mad for tomorrow's illumination

Verdant

a delicate orchestration
plays through green foliage overhead:

lie back in the grass

stare upward into the sun-dappled layers
of maple and elm, bird song and lore,
the scent of cut grass in the breeze

a shaded sort of feeling,
thoughts of quitting time on a Friday afternoon
in small nowhere neighborhoods
due east of the Hudson, west of Vermont,
with lawnmower vibrations still running
up the bones
stained knees,
hands, summer
daydreams of someday
coming back to this place with a better understanding
of all the ways in which bones grow thin and memories
unfurl across the miles

but in youthful summer doldrums
you can still smile,
get up off the earth, and rise
into blue infinity
with beautiful
ignorant hope

blooming in your chest

Southbound

She always chose a seat on the train that overlooked
the Hudson River going south, the right-hand side of
the car. The Amtrak seats squeaked all around her as
passengers sat and leaned back, the cloth of the seats
deep blue and wearing thin, the battleship gray of the
walls and armrest cool in the autumn afternoon. The
first thing she always did after sitting and situating
herself was to pluck out her hearing aids. And with
this, the world smoothed over into silence. No
squeaking chairs, no clattering luggage, no murmurous
conversations between strangers, no hum of the train
engine idling two cars ahead, only the gentle vibration
through the cool gray plastic walls.

In that silence, the world was her own, shaped by
curiosity and the sobering visions collected on her
endless trips south for work, for friends, for what she
couldn't always say. Maybe an endless desire to move
through space and time while she still had a little bit of
both in her life. Outside the train, she watched the sun
grappling with the Albany skyline, caught in the grip
of skyscrapers and cathedral steeples. The sun bled
yellow and peach and magenta across the horizon, but
along the edges of the sky she saw the peach-blood
sunset give way to deep blues and violet, the colors of
transition and sea change, if only temporary.

Her eyes shifted to a nearby building beside the
train tracks, familiar not because she knew what
happened within the structure but because she always
wondered what purpose it served. It stood just beyond
a chain link fence gnarled with ivy and sumac, beyond
a small blacktop parking lot riddled with lumps,
creases, potholes, and cracks, washed pale gray by time
and sunshine. The building looked like a small airplane
hangar, a half-cylinder of sheet metal with no signage

or hints to what lay within save for a small entryway halfway down one of its sloping, rippled sides streaked with rust. It didn't look dilapidated, necessarily. It looked…well, it looked mysterious and nostalgic, a building from another time that kept a foothold in that distant realm others could no longer reach.

What was this place? A business? Storage? In her muted wonderings she liked to imagine it was an old radio station, still broadcasting episodes of *Fibber McGee and Molly*, *The Shadow*, *Duffy's Tavern*, *Suspense*, *Night Beat*, and those lavish radio production of Orson Welles and his *Mercury Theatre*. She pictured a lonely DJ sitting at a desk cluttered with antiquated equipment, dials and knobs and flickering lights, headphones on a coiled cord, cigarette smoke curling up into a haze, and a hangar full of old recordings, sending those dark and antiquated tales out into the stars and latitudes unknown.

But in truth, she had no idea what happened in the hanger. All those times she passed through the train station, coming and going, she never saw anyone outside that old metal hangar, hemmed in by sumac bushes, scraggly oaks, piles of old pipes, and scrap metal. The parking lot was usually empty but there was a car there now, an old Buick, so there had to be someone who used the building. She'd never know. The train lurched gently, and in a few moments the hangar and the nearby brick buildings were behind her. If she closed her eyes in the silent rocking of the train car, she could almost see herself walking across that lot, opening the door, and stepping into the dark mystery within.

But she didn't see the door open. A man stepped out into the lot to watch the last of the train rumble-roll southbound out of the station. He lit a cigarette and blew a plume of silver into the air, coiling along the sides of the hangar, and he listened to the train in the distance heading toward Hudson, toward Rhinebeck, Poughkeepsie, and towns beyond. He'd never know just where that train went. He never rode one in his life and had no inclination, no need. He had work to do, far too much work to do.

Crushing the cigarette, he pulled the rusting metal door and returned to the old print shop within the hangar, the long tables and rolls of paper, the wooden pallets lining the walls stacked with machinery, inks, packaging, cut paper, twine, rubbish, layers and layers of dust, years and generations of it. Rows of tall metal shelving cast shadows thick and ubiquitous as they faded into the darkness of the hanger. He moved toward the other side of the open space, lit by a string of bare bulbs dangling from an unseen ceiling, looking for all the world like condemned men glowing at the end of a noose.

The man sat at a long flat table filled with paints and brushes, bottles of thinner and oil, stacks of canvas and works in progress drying in the light. To his left, an easel, heavy and scarred. His old companion, a stoic twin. He picked up a brush, tabbed the mixture of titanium white with a faint hint of alizarin crimson, and continued his work. Small gentle strokes into the recesses of hollow cheeks, the curvature of the ears, the wrinkles of the shirt, each strand of hair fading ever so slowly from the subject's brow. Now and then the man glanced at the mirror, then continued to paint his self-portrait.

The train slowed at the Hudson station, the crowds milling about in the evening dim, illuminated by lamplight and halogen, the engine rumbling. The woman woke and saw passengers waiting to exit, waiting to climb aboard, the conductor walking through calling out something she couldn't hear. In the silence she wondered what the station might have looked like years ago, fedoras and topcoats, cloche hats and Mary Janes, radio waves carrying tales of suspense through the autumn air. She thought of the hanger again and closed her eyes, as somewhere far behind her the hangar door opened once more.

The man looked up from his panting and felt a gentle dust-devil of autumn air following the man's nephew into the lit-up half of the hangar. They greeted one another and spoke of the weather and the boy's mother, and then the boy opened his notepad and began to write as the man returned to the array of oils and paints spread out before him. Now he used burnt umber. Then burnt sienna. Cerulean blue. Faint strokes of ivory black just along the edges here, there. A glance in the mirror. Now more white. Black again. A touch of crimson. The mirror. The incremental progeneration of his own visage on canvas. He glanced at his nephew hard at work and considered asking about his writing, but he knew to let it be until his nephew reached his destination, for the journey itself is for the traveler.

By the time the woman's train paused at Poughkeepsie, the two men stepped outside of the hanger for a break. The man lit a cigarette and watched low-hanging clouds slip by beneath the blues and purples of the night sky, ephemeral ghosts searching for new horizons. He strolled into the lot as dry leaves of copper and burgundy crackled and rolled all around them. The boy didn't smoke but he walked alongside his uncle, also gazing upward. He wrote poetry. He wrote novels. The novels, he said, never felt right, never said anything true enough. Some people wrote novels and they meant something. This one an allegory for overcoming loss. This one for surviving cancer. This one for the strength of the human heart under the pressure of relentless war. But the boy didn't know why he wrote anything. He saw people in his mind, saw them doing things, saw them fight and cry and struggle and wander and hope, but when agents and publishers said, "What does this mean in one sentence, in a ten second pitch?" Well, he wasn't sure. They were stories. They were complicated and maybe they didn't mean anything to anyone but him. Even then, the meaning wasn't always clear. Wasn't that life? Wasn't that what most people experienced day to day? The uncertainty of what it all means swallowing them whole?

"But that doesn't sell books," the man once told his nephew. The boy knew he was right but didn't know what to do about that. He could only write what came to him, and if what came to him wasn't marketable, was that enough reason to stop? Was that a reason to ignore the voices and events that appeared within his mind?

The man stubbed out his cigarette with his heel. He saw his nephew's silent misgivings and asked if he was okay. The boy said he was, only that he worried he wasn't getting anywhere with his writing. They watched the moon over the northern horizon and the uncle put his hand on the boy's shoulder and told him to keep going. "You only get somewhere when you arrive." The boy nodded. They went back inside.

When the train pulled into New York City, trundling past iron girders deep underground, people began to stand up and collect their bags. The woman waited. She felt no great hurry. Her next train southbound didn't leave for another hour. Not enough time to leave the station and too much time to sit without wondering what else might be going on in the great city surrounding her, calling to her. She considered putting her hearing aids back in, but they sometimes made her ears sore and what good came from incidental eavesdropping anyway? Her curiosity lived in what she saw, what she observed, so she sat in the embrace of her own singular silence and watched the other passengers begin to manage all their small responsibilities and intentions into a kinetic transformation as the train's doors opened. She waited, her silence so pure, and watched.

The man held his paint brush over the canvas and waited for that feeling of completion. Was he there? He stepped away from his painting and put his brush in the jar of muddy brown terpenoid to let the oils separate from the bristles, and he turned to the boy, who continued to write in his notebooks. Poems, stories, something in between, biographical, speculative, everything, whatever came to him. The man wondered if the boy would ever make the leap he desired. He wondered what would happen to his own paintings, unsold and stacked around him. He wondered if anyone ever found their destination or if it was all one long journey into night. He yawned and said he was finished.

The boy yawned too as he came around the table to look at the painting. It was beautiful if incomplete. Nothing is ever finished, even when the piece itself declares it has found its final form. They both understood that in their own unspoken way, but the boy told his uncle the painting was masterful. "Well, it's good enough, at least," the man said. He stepped further back, nodded at the painting, and reached for a rag to clean his hands, then his jacket. The boy was placing his notebooks into his bag. They knew the night was almost over. It would be cold out and the moon would hang high in the crisp October air. The man loved October, as did the boy. He turned out the lights and the two of them walked into the night.

Not long after, somewhere in the vast barren wetlands of central New Jersey, far from the lights of Manhattan, the train barreled southbound at top speed, the moonlight glinting off the water that occasionally appeared between thick rashes of cattails and reeds swaying in the autumn wind. The woman watched the scenes hurry by and wondered about the abandoned factory silhouette on the horizon. She wondered about the passing cars and trucks on the distant highway. She wondered about the sleeping woman in the seat across from her. Where were they all going and why? We're all moving in space toward someplace, she thought, toward something, and the answer will either present itself in a moment of fulfillment or one of devastating regret. The truth of a journey waits for each of us at our destination, and in the meanwhile, we move forward, as does the moon above, followed by the sun and days and nights that chased it across the horizon in astral silence.

Ruins

the mighty will fall,
the supple will bend in any wind

outside the train window through a sheen
of river fog in dawn's awakening
stands the crumbling remains of the island castle,
the old Bannerman armory ages old, tattered
by war and time and torrential rains,
history and mother nature gripping
the stones and towers with vine and root
to pull it down to the water, down to the rising
brush and reeds, an embrace not unlike lovers
during apocalyptic winter nights, succumbing
to fate and fatality, lust born in weary silver mist
at dawn, sweeping over the river skin, over and over
and over again as passing specters through train
windows watch and whisk southbound to endless seas
and skies and time ticking away on its infinite fingers:

love me // love-me-not // love me

until that fallen pile of stone returns to clay
far behind us

but to have ended is not to have disappeared
to retain a semblance is not to keep a structure

to see without being seen,
mere breathless filaments away
from what it means to exist and love
to be; without

we are all such ruins
we are all worthy of such an embrace

once mighty, now supple
                    succumb

White Wicker

sit in the white wicker furniture
with me in the middle of Pine Avenue
and stare through the maple leaves
and power lines crisscrossing overhead
into the stars and the clouds draping
themselves over the moonlight

share your dreams as the hum from
Western Avenue washes over us
in white noise pulsations with spectral
headlights dancing through the elms

tell the shadows every secret you keep hidden
from the sun sleeping out there across the
horizon, past the Catskills and Rockies
and the reticent Pacific beyond them

lean back in that white wicker furniture
beside me, carried to the middle of Pine
Avenue, and hold my hand as the traffic
fades to silence, as the stars blink out, and
whisper your final wish as I whisper mine
in ephemeral unison, then close your eyes

as time lifts us up, and sets us down into
that realm where the sway of the trees
and the pollen drifting in the springtime
air are the only lines of communication
we will need to know each other's heart

Unrequited

this water is too cold
but my body numbs to it
as I bob and float and touch
the side of the pool with my
fingertips

night is the time
to swim

and I am weightless
in the invisible water,

a spaceman,
a ghost

no need for memory
no need for gravity
no need for corporeal filaments of matter
no need for shining quarters to bring me home
no need for anything beyond this dark upstate cascade

a spaceman
a ghost

this water is my air and death
complete

I dip below the surface,
open the visor,
and take in the darkness of the universe
as crickets dance
through the spectral grass
and starlight

The Place Where Waters Are Never Still

I sense your pulse
no matter where
I place my fingers

into the soft earth,
or along the edges
of the cold cement
sidewalk in the middle
of the night, lit only
by the single lamppost
somewhere behind me

I close my eyes and
the years peel away,
taking the traffic lights
and the theater marquee
and the steel towers
with them, the scent of
exhaust and refuse
dissipating to crisp air
and wet soil, moldering
yellow leaves in the
underbrush of fall

there are histories we
will never teach in school,
that there were once greater
majesties than our fables,
that there were languages
once spoken through these
hollows that will never
carry desires through the
summer breeze again

even the silence that came
before the original heartbeat
was a sort of holiness we will
never be able to bottle and
sell, two-day delivery for
special customers only

while in the here and now, cars are
double parked all up and down
Central Avenue, where the red lights
always get you when you're in
a hurry trying to make a movie
on time or return some pants

aerial bombardment and
hate on the radio, chaos on every
app and social platform
while we laugh and laugh
and chant and chant
and cry and cry and
scream into the void of
our own creation as we
run headlong into knives
and burning oil and endless death

when we are gone
and
there is no one left
to honk
at jaywalkers on Central
Avenue
and only the weeds
and insects and dandelions
and blackbird
remain to sing
the hymnals of the only faith

that truly matters, the only
existence that means anything,
the great nothing that came
before us and might yet
come again after every human
impulse is put to clay

when that day comes, there
might yet be a pulse, a heartbeat

if you set your fingers just so
into the cool damp earth
in the place where the waters
are never still

you'll feel it, and you'll know
we were all wrong to come here
and take what can never be given,
only to replace it with something
so unholy, so unkind, so human

the great hulking
timebomb of Us

Driver Dave

he drove my Toyota backward
all the way through Greenwich

I followed him on foot, such a
lonely parade at 11 p.m. at night

past empty churches, empty gazeboes,
empty parks and banks and schools,

two cars in the K-Mart parking lot and
Stewart's selling half-price ice cream

a small farm town on the edge of
nowhere, the clutch long gone

the only gear that stilled worked
was reverse, so he said he'd do it

I thought it was too crazy to try myself,
but he made it, 5 mph the whole way

Dave, browbeaten by life, living in a rented
room after his wife asked for a separation

though not a divorce, that was too much,
too final, too sad, but he'd never return

he'd spend the rest of his days driving
backward through his life, slow and crazy

willing to try anything, nothing to lose,
later stealing my car from the mechanic's lot

when the mechanic tried to screw me over,

leaving burn-out ruts in the muddy lawn

the mechanic calling me, screaming for his bill,
but Dave said, *forget him, he doesn't know anything*

and returned to his rented room to drink alone
as I listened to the phone ring and wonder what to do

my muddy car hiding under a tarp, the clutch gone,
and so many miles ahead of me with no way forward

Hibernation

foxtail breath silver and running
into winter skies fraught with roil,
starless, cloudful, impending ice
storms in pellet infidelities that
peck away at whatever comforts
we've accrued to shield ourselves
from such misfortune: inevitable

hooded figures hustle down State
Street, discarded Christmas trees in
inchoate dreams, silent envelopment
as the sudden snow formulates into
view and amasses in thin choirs along
curbs, between cobbles, shoulders
of children and parents hurrying
inside with groceries, backpacks,
shovels at the ready to forge hope
out of crystalline noir powdered
across the cityscape lamppost night

watching from the second story
bedroom window, curtains drawn
closed, baseboards ticking their
thermal threat, we descend into
sheets, comforters, feather and
down duvets in clean hues of pink
to shiver cool our bare skin until
rhubarb red lamp light slips into the
sheets, filtered through pink, down
into our den where hearts and lungs
pulse vulpus wild through the night
holding tight to arctic assurances and
the hope for warmer seasons beyond

Northern Dominion

new moon divinations
  sink into the teeth of the world,
into the jagged evergreen treeline
drowning in silent lore

the canoe eases back to shore
almost no paddle needed, little insects
  dancing on the surface of the lake,
fires dotting the horizon

the embers of kindness burning low

in the rose-gold hush, a memory ebbs:
home and you and how your silence
  could sooth the fevered hours
the night made soft by your very breath

but the embers are burning low
for everyone these days

this world is not long for any of us
  and soon that peaceful silence that once was
and will forever be upon our departure
will run desolation wild

dominion born anew

Is This Really Necessary?

there were three doctors with knives
and I kept asking, "Is this really
necessary?" and the one dermatologist
who watched from the back kept
asking me if Lake Placid was in
the Catskills because he was thinking
of vacationing there, and that was
near Albany, right?

as the other doctor cut into my forearm with a knife

he did warn me at one point not
to open my eyes, but I did, and saw
the blood all over the sheets, my
gown, the stitches not quite stitched,
the gore blinking at me

Central Park in April is a calming
consolation prize as your body
tries to eat itself—the ducks, the
cool breeze over the lake, the sun,
the blood leaking from the gauze

they used to sail boats in a stone pond
in Central Park and I remembered
that one famous writer who included a scene
about the pond in that immortal book of his,
but things probably look different now
and very little in life feels immortal, much
less the words of a dead man,
all of his lines and all of mine
just fire in the flood

nobody looks at you or your bandages

on the northbound train, nobody cares;
we are all looking away from
one brand of gore or another, trying
our best to ignore the small hand
of the clock spinning into midnight
where new doctors wait with
knives like you've never seen

and they won't listen to your questions either

You're No Bukowski

Down by the Greyhound station in Albany you'll find
an open wound, a gaping maw of near-empty parking
lots hemmed in by chain-link fences as ragged and
cockeyed against the wind as cattails in a marsh.
Weeds frill through every crack in the busted asphalt.
Highway onramps curl into the night sky. Many a night
have I walked to the bus station, or home after a long
trip, always traveling as cheaply as I could. As I
walked through the empty lots that night, I could see
the dented taxi cabs waiting in line beside the station,
the drivers smoking in a circle and telling jokes. I
could hear them laughing from more than fifty yards
away, their voices carried by the wind buffeting up
from the Hudson River.

I wasn't catching a Greyhound that night. I had
agreed to meet someone I only knew from social
media, another writer, a kid out of Oregon making his
way to Boston, hopping cities and visiting all the
writers he said he admired from the small press world.
The kid, Westin Lee Browder (everyone just called
him Wes), had worked his way to Philly, then New
York City, and now he wanted to see me for some
reason, a quick three-hour bus ride to Albany before
cutting east for his final leg. He'd been posting about
his trek on Facebook and it reminded me of my
excitement when devouring *On The Road* at eighteen
and wanting to just *GO*. Wes was about twenty-two, a
few years younger than I was when I first hit the road,
so out of nostalgia I was a little curious to hear how it
was going for him. The least I could do was buy the
kid a beer. He said he'd get in around 6:15 pm and
would have to leave again by 8:30 when his transfer
arrived, so I replied to his Facebook message saying he

83

could meet me at the Parish House on Broadway, a three-minute walk from the station.

The Parish was supposed to be a "New Orleans bar" but it didn't look much different than any typical Irish pub in the northeast, with bare brick walls inside, dark wood stools and tables, a couple televisions, a dart machine, the same cheap beer on tap they had anywhere, and it was pretty quiet on a Wednesday night. Most bar-crawlers in town were up on Pearl Street or Lark if they were out that early at all. By the time Wes left town again later that night, the college crowds would likely begin to line up outside Pearl Street Pub or Stout, which sounded like Irish pubs but were actually nightclubs with DJs, crowded dance floors, and cheap drinks served in red plastic cups all night. City Beer Hall had a mechanical bull and free pizza. Legends was wall-to-wall TVs showing college sports. Lionheart drew the college frat-bros. None of those were my scene, and the Parish was closer to the station anyway, a perfect spot for a couple writers to get to know one another.

When I walked in, he was at the bar alone, a short kid with an unkempt beard, travel-worn clothes that probably hadn't been laundered since crossing the Mississippi, and a walking stick as tall as he was leaning against the counter. The place was almost empty, just four or five other people at far tables. I pulled the stool next to him and introduced myself. He almost leapt up to greet me, humming with kinetic eagerness, his handshake too strong, making me wonder if he'd ingested something other than a Budweiser.

"It's really awesome to meet you, man. Sit down, sit down. You look just like your photo, you know that?"

"Well I hope so," I said, then ordered a Becks. "How was the ride up?"

"Horrible, man. I'm so sick of busses. You can't sleep right, nobody wants to talk to you, the john in the back stinks all the time, it's the worst. I walked halfway here you know. Really. I walked pretty much from Eugene to Boise, took a bus until Nebraska and started walking again, just to avoid people looking at me funny all the damn time, walked a bunch through Indiana, Ohio, then all busses again. See these shoes? Worn right through, man. Holes in both. But I won't change them 'til I get to Boston. That's a promise. Did you know they have by-the-hour hotels in New York City? With real hookers hanging out inside?"

"Yeah, there's still some pockets of old New York around."

"You lived there, right?"

"I did. Queens and Brooklyn for five years, then I was done. I served my time and came home."

"You came back here? Serious?"

"Albany's not so bad. It's like anywhere—it's what you make of it."

"You ever stay in those by-the-hour places? I did for three nights. The bed had a vibrating machine you start with quarters and they had a mirror above the bed. I'd lay there naked and jack—"

"Hey, I don't need to know that."

The kid laughed and started to tell me about a woman from Venezuela he met at a strip club in Hell's Kitchen, and how he went to the same place each night to try to talk to her and get her to come back to his by-the-hour room.

"Never could convince her though. Looked like a porn star. My loss. Couldn't take my eyes off her. Hey, I liked your piece in *Gutter Eloquence Magazine*. The poem about the rats in the subway and all the Saturday night drunks going home on the N train. Where did you drink in the city? Anywhere cool?"

"I wouldn't call it cool, just a place in the Bowery. Bleecker Street Bar. They had pool tables in the back—"

"I liked your poem in *Red Fez* too, the one about some bar in San Antonio and the guy with the knife. Shit, you and me, we been all over. We should do a road trip together, man. How many women you hook up with down there in Texas?"

"Well..."

He spared me having to think of an answer by steamrolling me with descriptions of his travels through the Rockies and the women who rejected him along the way, the stories of bar fights and flights from cops, and as he told me how he spent the night sleeping behind a bar until it opened, it dawned on me that I shouldn't believe at least eight out of ten things he said. I was trying to decide if he was trying to impress me or if he was just this way naturally when he started talking about a girl he met at the Greyhound station in Cincinnati and how she wouldn't join him in the bathroom. He had to leave the bus station for a while because she told a cop about him. *That* story I believed. Then he went on about the poets he met in Kansas City and Cleveland, how cool the underground scenes were there, and how much he hated New York City.

"Everyone is rude as shit. I tried to sit with some people in this restaurant and they were real assholes."

"Well, people anywhere would think that was rude," I said. I talked about my life in the city and his eyes stared, almost unblinking, small hard almonds of black with a piercing antagonism, reminding me of a long walk I took one night before coming across a stray dog, how it stared at me, deciding in its primal animal brain if I was worth the fight, if I was worth chasing down, latching onto with diseased teeth. Wes smiled, but those eyes never lost that look of hard amusement.

"How's your writing going?" I asked, attempting to steer the conversation toward calmer waters. "You got stuff in *Zygote*, didn't you?"

"Yeah, I've been lucky lately, I went from nothing to showing up everywhere but what does it all mean? Nobody reads it." He kicked back his Budweiser and wiped his lips in his sleeve. "The only people who read poetry are poets and half of them fake it. I think people only want to get published, brag about it, post their work, and start all over again. It's a big stupid game. A bunch of phonies. I don't really believe anyone reads anything they're published in. And when's the last time you heard of anyone reading poetry who didn't write it too? It's all bullshit."

"So why do it then?"

"Good question."

"Well..."

"What else am I going to do?" He downed the last of his beer and ordered another, and two shots of Jameson. "You have a job?"

"Yeah, a day job editing for an education pub—"

"Oh man, no, that's cheating."

"What? No it's not. I have bills to pay, medical—"

"Yeah but I'm saying, all the greats, you didn't see them stuck in an office. You didn't see them selling their soul for a few bucks and a cozy bed and no time left to write like a chump. Can you see Neal Cassady in an office, or—"

"Neal Cassady had a ton of jobs. And he didn't really write."

"—Kerouac, Bukowski, Gary Snyder, or—"

"Bukowski worked in a post office. Kerouac lived with his mother half his life. I don't know what you mean by having a job is cheating."

"It just doesn't seem right, man. It's not pure. Not real."

"Nobody lives on poetry alone."

"Some guys do. Dorsey does. You know Dorsey?"

"John Dorsey works his ass off," I said. "If he can live off the poems, then he earned it. I can't do that. Most of us can't do that."

Wes brushed that away with a wave of his hand. "Listen, I lived with a girl once, just a few months, and all I did was write. It was the best time of my life. I wrote the best stuff. Objectively the best. About love and death and reality. About *her* even. And she threw me out! Can you believe that? Everything I've written since has been rough, man. You can write about skid row a whole lot better when you're not still there. She just left me in the cold. But it's better than being a fucking fraud sitting in an office all day writing bar poems."

He stared at me as the shots of Jameson arrived. I was about to say something in my defense but I laughed instead, an insecure laugh that sounded as much even to my own ears. I didn't want to have this conversation because it felt so childish, so petulant. It reminded me of friends I had who held tight to political idealism and the absurd disdain for anything that fell short of their absolute doctrine. There was no middle ground, no concession.

He raised his shot glass and said, "Here's to the real ones." He waited for me to raise mine too, which I did after a moment. We threw them back.

"Next round, you toast. Two more shots please."

The bartender nodded but continued making a cocktail for someone else. I hesitated, struggling to think of something else to say as we waited, and then I nodded to his walking stick.

"What's with that? You hike much?"

"My uncle gave me that, pure redwood. See this," he pulled the stick close. In its polished veneer I saw six notches. "One for every girl I hooked up with on this trip. Boise, Cheyanne, Kansas City, St. Louis, Toledo, and Philly. You ever been in love?'

"Once or twice."

"What's that like? Being in love?"

He asked with such unexpended tenderness that it gave me pause. I thought for a moment.

"When it's working," I said, "nothing can touch it. You're elevated. Everything you've known becomes new again."

"What do you mean?"

"Songs and books and movies, places you go, food, you see it through their eyes and it's reborn into something better, something you can share. You're eager to share it, every simple little thing takes on new meaning, because of them. But it's deeper than that. It's ephemeral. Their existence becomes engrained into your every waking moment. But, on the other hand, when it doesn't work, nothing—"

"I don't believe in love."

"What?'

"It's like carving out a piece of your flesh and handing it to someone. You ain't getting that back no matter what happens. I believe people lust after each other and have a good time with each other but the idea of love is pretty stupid."

"Okay…if that's how you see it."

"And if you were in love, why aren't you anymore?"

"Things change."

He scoffed. "Doesn't that mean you were wrong?"

"Not necessarily. Sometimes the thing that changes isn't you, it's them."

The shots arrived and he raised his glass, his eyes piercing mine, dark and glinting in the neon.

"Well?" he asked.

I picked mine up. "To the women we've loved, and the ones we might yet love."

I downed mine and saw he was still holding his, his lips curling into a cruel smile.

"You're soft. Softer than I thought you'd be."

"What?"

"You're no Bukowski."

"Who said I was?"

"You act like it online," he said. "All this hobo stuff, bar poems, being on the road. You're not hard at all."

"I never tried to be hard."

"You're disappointing."

With that I pushed my chair back to leave but he grabbed my forearm.

"You can't get offended, man. It's just how I feel. The internet is fake as shit and we all fall victim to it. We're different online. Can't help it. I am too probably. Everyone is. It's a fantasy world. But you aren't anything like you project yourself to be."

"I'm not—look, sure, people are different online, and there are a lot of Bukowksi knockoffs out there, but—"

"Oh, and you're not?"

"No. Bukowski is Bukowski," I said, "And Plath is Plath, O'Hara is O'Hara, Dorsey is Dorsey, I'm me and you're whoever you are. Frankly, at twenty-two, you probably don't even know who you are yet."

"And when I'm thirty-something like you, I will?"

"Hopefully you will. And hopefully it won't be whoever this is. And yeah, I like Bukowksi, he got me into poetry, but people should be aiming higher than him. A lot higher. He's fine but there's better. And as for me, I don't want to be anyone but me. Not him, not you, just me."

"Don't get mad," Wes said. "Relax, we're just talking shop, man. This is what we do, we drink, we talk poetry, we have a good time. You're super sensitive, man. I had no idea. Besides, I still want to go barhopping together. I still respect your work, man."

"You have a bus to catch."

"No I don't."

I stared at him for a long moment. "What?"

"I didn't buy a ticket yet. I can crash with you as long as you like."

"I don't have the space," I said. "I have a basement studio. I don't even have a couch."

"Oh c'mon."

"I'm serious, there's nowhere—"

"No, no, I mean, c'mon, you're too nice," he laughed. "Just say no. I can take it."

"Okay, no."

"Was that so hard? And now you're just like everyone else in my life. I didn't expect different, so don't feel bad."

"Bad for what?"

He laughed a little as he sipped his beer, then leaned toward me, lowered his voice. "One day I'm going to be remembered for things you only dream of. I'm going to be one of the greats, and you'll be nobody."

I didn't know what to say. I just shook my head, drank my Becks, and looked up to see myself in the mirror behind the bar, a head floating above bottles of vodka and gin. I saw a mid-thirties writer laid off from three magazine jobs in a row, who left New York City penniless to return to his hometown, a bad back, gray in his beard, six unpublished novels, and an empty studio apartment that flooded every time it rained too hard. I sipped the last of my Becks and stood up.

"Look, kid. Greatness is the most subjective thing in the world, and I don't think I want anything to do with your kind of greatness."

"God you poets are so goddamn delicate!" he called after me as I walked out the door. Before I reached the end of the block, I heard the door open up and his walking stick clack-clack on the sidewalk after me. He shouted, "C'mon man, let's have a cigarette and walk around for a while! Stop! You're too good to act like this!"

But I didn't stop. At the next block I looked back. He was standing where I left him, smoking and leaning against a lamppost watching me. He looked like a kid waiting for a ride after a three-day music festival out in the boondocks, his pants muddy, his t-shirt collar loose around his neck with weeks of grime. He smiled like nothing happened at all, like the world and all its possibilities was a great big joke. He waved. I waved back. Then I turned the corner and never saw him again.

He sent three messages that night, one saying he found a bar with a mechanical bull. Later he said he met some girls and I should come out. Then around eleven at night he sent a message that he was on a bus to Boston, the last one out of town, and that he was happy to have met me. But I was soft and I should read Bukowski to remember why I started this life in the first place.

This life. What did he know about this life, this city, or anything? I read his message again and glanced over at my poetry books stacked on the floor and considered all the poets out there wandering those books like ghosts, winnowing down their idea of greatness until it defined only a small collective that sounded just like them. And maybe I was like that too, but I hoped I wasn't. I turned out the light and opened the kid's Facebook page. I felt bad for a moment, but I blocked him then powered off my phone. If the kid wanted to go out like Neal Cassady, let him walk those railroad tracks in Mexico all by his lonesome. Let him have greatness. I had writing to do.

Wednesday Sunset South Main Ave

you know why
the light fades from the sky
the sand sinks in the tide
far below me

you know where
the ghosts go when we sleep
somewhere in the deep
far below me

I can't take
the ways the hours burn
the way my luck won't turn
back to face you

I can't hide
from fevers in my mind
from midnight love maligned
from all these ropes that bind
and keep me from you

but when the sun burns down
on the distant edge of town
I hope you'll come around
looking for me

and I'll be here
waiting in the night
the distant summer lights
shining for us

A Molting Thing in Transition

growing up in a rural trailer park
left much to be desired
    an outcast anywhere I went,
mocked in the neighborhood
for books I'd carry instead
of stolen cigarettes or NASCAR
numbers on my backpack,
    and at school they'd ask me
if we ate our food stamps if we
got too hungry
or they'd ask how it felt
to walk around shoeless
in the summertime ringworm
afternoons in the trailer park

I can still feel the imprint
of their fists in my stomach
when I had nothing
to say in return

isolation is easy to find:
riding my bike through
rutted trails to corn fields,
orchards, the pine barrens beyond,
sliding to a halt and sitting
beside a creek, miles
from the nearest farmhouse,
watching the water glint
sunlight, trickle over stones,
the tall grass wicking my legs,
the leaves burnt sienna and rattling,
cattails in the breeze,
ants crawling over a dead
robin in the wildflowers

its beak and bones and skull
lying in bleached white contrast to the
freedom it once had, but
now it is like me
   a molting thing in transition

on full moon October evenings
I sometimes ruminate through the years
and re-discover those dirt paths
that lead to the forest somewhere
beyond the corn fields filled with
   yellow clattering bones
and along that old creek
I sit and think of what could
have been, what may yet be,
what I could still choose to become
when it is time to make the transition

maybe I'm talking about Halloween
maybe I'm talking about life
maybe the masks we wear are chosen
maybe they never come off

what I do know now is that
   it's closer to the end of the night
than it is the previous dawn

so in a few moments I will rise
and walk into those Albany streets,
who I was and who I am melding
into who I could be, a mask
smiling and screaming as time
bleeds out October rust,
   the chances thinning but liking
my chances as I try my best to be
kind, to be humble, to complete

the transmutation before
   my bones lie in wait for
the sun to bleach them
clean into my final perfect state

Kaleidoscope

the sort of night where he makes you wear his
sunglasses while he drives and loudly recalls
that scene from Fear & Loathing about the
merry-go-round bar and the polar bear, Hunter
trying to purchase a monkey; orange spastic lights
up and down Troy at night, the bars, the traffic,
trying to find a pool table, trying to skirt the
checkpoints, ride the crest of adrenochrome until
we get home, sunglasses intact, the colors of
the spinning universe alight no matter how you
close your eyes, and you can still hear him laughing
downstairs on the livingroom floor, too weird to live,
and too soon we'll all die, gone to dust in a desert
and all these memories evaporating into the night

Where Fun Goes to Die

Like any hometown, there's nothing more I wanted than to escape the same staid streets and supermarkets, the sad, fading strip malls and gas stations, and when people asked me where I came from I'd always tell them it was the grayest city in America, where fun goes to die. But I found death elsewhere, too. After I helped my grandmother out of her bathtub, after falling with two broken arms, and eased her down into her grave, the southwest Texas winds cast daredevil whirlwinds of dust through the funeral home parking lot and I felt a panic in my heart. I loaded the back seat of my car with all I owned and drove northeast until the prairie grass turned to pine and snow, and sometimes I dream about what it would be like if I never left the south, and sometimes I wonder what it would be like if I went west instead, palm trees and forest fire summers. But I am here, one mile from the hospital where I was born, a nearly completed circle, but it's not a prison or a shame, it's an arrow through time, steel tipped and feathered, flying into a high arc, peaking in the clear blue springtime skies, and someday falling down, down, into the soft dirt and moss shaded by Japanese maples and willowy pines that lines this quiet street, the lamppost lights my pallbearers, the gentle midnight breeze my last rites, the lights of the movie-house marquee glimmering through the shadows just down the street my gathered loved ones, sending me into the unknown fathoms to join the rest of the cosmos, my grandmother, my dreams, in that great hometown beyond all reckoning and remembrance.

Both Ways Home

be it roughshod in the back
of a mini-van adorned with Phish
stickers, piled in with drums
and sleeping guitarists, or

hungover after Ithaca nights,
bourbon madness on motel
balconies tossing poems back and
forth with ol' Joe Hoffer, or

aiming for Albany after melancholic
nights wandering Nashville alone,
Little Rock alone, Texarkana alone,
hoping for yet another restart, or

swinging back to Texas, aiming the old
Ford through the first brush of winter,
down through Harrisburg to see ol'
Joe Hoffer, a younger incarnation, or

looking for bookstores on a Sunday,
looking for wineries on a Saturday,
looking for Jesse's old station wagon,
tire blown out at 11:14 p.m., or

who the hell knows what else, this gouge
in New York's hide of mountains and ruts,
sweeping valleys and old boom towns now
rusted out to their brick-and-marrow, and

I know it won't be the last time next time,
and maybe not even after that, but even
if it is, ol' Highway 88 hasn't been so bad,
even with its potholes from hell following me

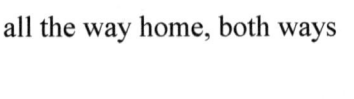

all the way home, both ways

Perennial

reckless ascension through rough earth
hewn by hand, stalks rising from bulbs
blooming yellow and red and white, just
as they have for centuries in this park
once surrounded by Dutch colonial
shanties—and eons before that, hollows
and hillocks of elm, maple, pine

my life rose in such places, blue skies
and lustrous white sheets of cirrus
spanning the springtime horizon,
blossoms new to the air all red and
yellow and white, and in the years
afterward I crossed the river there
down the hill back and forth like
stitching a wound, the years flowing
away from me, hiding so much
from sight, carrying so much away

and each spring the bulbs twist
in the wild earth of sprawling
Washington Park and rise like that,
radiate through summer hours,
heat wave quotidian, showers and
moonfall inconsolable, and then
come the cool winds of autumn

people say they live lifetimes in just one,
and sometimes that feels true, chapters
turned from one to the next and so many
of the characters fall through the lines,
slip into the spine, lost to pulp, faded ghosts,
and like so many of them I begin again, Chapter
Ten, Chapter Thirty, Chapter Fifty-Five...

pages filled on idle summer days in the park

where knees push into the dirt and red leaves
fall from maples, from elms, and city workers
burrow into the earth with their hands and
small metal spades and bury hard brown bulbs
down in the soil, covering and watering each
mound, patting the earth flat and looking
into the cascading transcendence above, a
small silent prayer before rising to their feet
and leaving the dried husks below to
the hard embrace of winter

sometimes I see a paperback novel
left to rot beneath a park bench or
beside a garbage can, dead dandelions
sulking beside the waterlogged pages,
and as the river passes by in the valley
below and as the sun sets in the distant
horizon, the pages dissolve into earth,
as will I when the second and minute
and hour hands of my heartbeat slow,
and stop, and when they do I hope to
feel the rough hands of the city workers
parting the soil and setting me deep
into the earth beneath blue autumn
skies, and they don't even have to
say a prayer for me because I know
what the seasons will bring if I'm
patient enough to wait

SAN ANTONIO, TEXAS

Bar America

I've heard that tower rotates and
I've heard there's a restaurant at
the top that's just a glorified Jim's
Diner, or overpriced seafood, but
I've never been up there to find out
despite the fact it has dominated
this city's skyline for my entire life

from down here, in some alleyway
near Bar America on a Friday night,
it looks like a monument to eternity,
a pawn shop Eifel Tower aglow in
orange neon afterburn and dust

and from within the bar the clacking
of the pool tables and the smell of
Lone Star beer draws me back,
a calmer evening now that we are
able to communicate with the
Mexican Nationals who came in
looking for a fight when they found
us at their pool table, insistent eyes
and steely jaws, all of our high school
Spanish failing us until some regular
stepped in and explained, and half
an hour later we were all buying
each other dollar beers and grinning
even though we still needed a translator,
but that's how it goes some nights, the
world spinning madly as towers grip
the concrete earth beneath, and all
of us wandering beyond borders and
language just trying to hunker down
and distract ourselves with drinks

and games and temporary companionship
until, like every tower eventually, we
too fall to dust, crumble beneath our
own weight and expectations, leaving
a gap in the horizon of someone else's
night only filled by stars, that orange neon
glow, and the sounds of a bar calling
them to come inside and wait for their turn

Saint Michael
(for Stray)

in that little stucco apartment
built around 1947 with all its age-old
charms and Spanish tile awnings,
you'd cook dinner and set out
the chess board, talk to me
in the cool shade beneath purple
phosphorescent skies

you monk, you brother,
you taoist, you friend,
offering confession and communion,
black bean tacos and beer;
what will I do without these memories?
I'd crawl all the way back through time
on my hands and knees to make them again,
to move the pawns and rooks in
and out of danger as you smiled and
waited for your turn to show me
the way

Dead City Jazz

the night will come when the music stops
and the city goes dark to my heart

once the fire of my bloodline embers down
to coals that throb and cool and harden to black
in the coming gusset of dawn, what will remain
for me in that tangle of concrete and neon?

ancestors gone, aunts and uncles, my father
tending the grandfather clock passed down
to the end of the line where dust gathers
in the back room beside the old wooden
radio from Depression-Era homesteads, still
lighting up when the dials turn, soft whispers
from the past, dead city jazz ebbing from ages
lost to mahogany and silk, six feet of soil

I'll tell you what remains: desperation
for the nights of whiskey on ice in dive
bars scattered across the city, the rush from
one to the next, the eagerness for arrival
and the excitement of departure to find
friends at the next tavern, love in the back room,
pool tables clicking in green lights, darts in red,
jukebox thunder and laughter for miles

and then you wake in a cool white room
lifetimes down the line, far from youthful
indiscretion and stupid mistakes, but mistakes
that led you to a better place, a safer place,
a place of soft arms and warm lips in the
pre-dawn light as you wonder what ghosts
you'll find if you look back too much, or at all

but no matter what cool, calm, safe place you find,
you know last call is just a reprieve, and when
that final bell tolls and the embers cool to black,
when your father hands you the key to tend that
wooden clock dressed in cobwebs, the radio
will fade, the jazz will die, the tangle of highways
with straighten to one road leading home
north by northeast, back to pine and snow
with San Antonio and all the ghosts it can muster
far behind now, burning and glowing until I too
cool to endless ash on that last night of dead city jazz

strange gods of the prairie

in the south Texas night across
vast plains sloping gradient toward the sea,
towers of emaciated steel wait in the dark, calling
out with pulsating lights, mendicant prayers
offered toward passing cars and trucks
on yonder highway heading south toward
the coastal towns or northward into
the city of San Antonio, an orange dome
of light on the horizon

the towers flash in sequence, little thunderbolts
at midnight separated by barbed wire,
hard yellow dirt, tumbleweed and stone
and the forever hours between dusk and dawn,
begging the little glowing insects on that highway
yonder
to peel away from their journey to join them
in the immense nothingness

beyond the stars and the moon and the
sweeping horizon, the towers stare off toward the cities
of the plain, sights they'll never see,
burning sources of power sucking their lifeforce away
through cables and wire, leaving them
erect and alone towering over fields of dead cotton
and rusted, oily pumpjacks turning idle
in the hot wind

their morse code refrain
their pleading flash of white
their unrequited dream of more
of elsewhere

the cars and trucks pass by in the night

and children watch from windows, watch the
flickering lights, ask their parents what it all means,
only
to hear hoarse whispers from the front seat:
go on now, back to sleep, there are miles
to go before home

then nothing but miles of night
small trailers with television antennae
stucco homes along a crippled arroyo
closed gas stations of black neon

then looping highway ramps
a billboard for divorce lawyers
a bbq franchise with one car in the drive-through

the subtle signs of a city rising
against the tide of night,
the orange dome now surrounding
those highway travelers and dreaming children,
some of them forgetting all they'd seen
on their long journey,
and some of them dreaming still,
of that pulsing call in the night, a language
they could not translate but understood deep
in their marrow, their synapses,
a proclamation from strange gods of the prairie
standing alone in the night and waiting their chance
for a future all their own

Afternoons in Bulverde

Even in the summertime, there's a brief period in the mornings in Texas hill country when it's cool, or at the very least calm and shady, and in that early respite John would take his coffee on the porch. It was a small cottage in the center of Bulverde, an aging cluster of clapboard homes and small businesses of stucco and yellow cement nestled into a low flat hollow of bedrock and cacti, stubborn saltgrass and squat oak trees. One twisting blacktop road led east toward Highway 281 a few miles away, though at this point 281 was just one lane in either direction. If you took it south toward San Antonio it eventually widened to two lanes as you began to pass new housing developments, then shopping centers and strip malls, gas stations and exit ramps, and then it widened to three as you entered the city proper toward downtown, a heated tangle of concrete and steel reaching into the pale blue sky.

But out toward Bulverde, the little village down that twisting road a few miles from 281, you couldn't even hear the traffic, could barely imagine it. And as he sipped his coffee, he heard only the soft sway of the wind rattling the leaves in the gnarled oaks.

In the morning, he wrote. Nothing too great most days, but good enough to keep the lights on and keep the refrigerator somewhat full of milk, eggs, bacon, Lone Star beer, okra and other fresh produce when needed. It was his fifteenth western and it was going slowly ever since he decided to add elements of a murder mystery to this one, for flair. He had to go back to the start to do so, but around 11:30 each morning he'd slow down and by noon he'd take this third coffee out onto the porch, the sun high and the heat really pouring down now. Even in the shadow of the porch, his skin shivered as the oppressive warmth cooked his

113

body. He sipped his coffee and looked across the street, catching a glimpse of her in the post office window.

Molly had worked in the post office for about as long as John had lived in Bulverde, going on two decades now. He could still call himself young back then, for a little while longer at least, an upstart with a two-book deal under his belt and his third off to his editor. All he wanted was a quiet place to get away from Austin and San Antonio, away from universities and students, the papers to grade and the grousing of frustrated young writers. He found it in Bulverde.

So did Molly. She started working young to take care of her mom, leaving school as soon as it was legal to do so. When the cancer won, Molly moved in with a young man who promised her bouquets and warm nights on the Texarkana prairie. But he drank and watched TV and yelled at her about laundry and even at 19 she knew this wasn't the life she wanted, so she left to find anything else. She found work in a post office in Fort Worth, then Waco, and then Bulverde, always aiming for something smaller, quieter, further away from anything that looked like home.

The same autumn John moved to Bulverde, Molly began selling stamps and weighing parcels at the desk just out of sight of the big glass window facing John's cottage. By Christmas she moved to the other counter when Peggy Howitzer retired, and whenever he'd sip his coffee on his porch swing, he'd see her counting out stamps for a customer or sorting mail into the wall of PO boxes.

He remembered the morning she noticed him, when he first waved. She waved back, a small one with a smile. Not a day went by when they didn't wave to one another through that window, even after they married a few years later. Save for Sundays, this is, when the post office was closed. On Sundays she'd make chicken fried steak and he'd make fried okra and mashed potatoes and if it was cool enough outside they'd eat on the back porch together, facing away from the twisting road and the post office and the other dozen homes and shops in the center of dusty little Bulverde. They'd drink iced tea and talk about the day, then she'd putter with her flowers and wind chimes. He'd fix the one crooked rail in the back fence that kept slipping sideways. They owned a TV but didn't use it much. With the library three doors down, why bother?

She'd read in bed. He read on the couch with his knees tucked beneath him until he almost fell asleep, and then he'd rise and join her in bed, where he'd read half a page more and fall asleep for good. She'd turn off the lights for them both and would be gone in the morning when he woke.

The afternoons were long in Bulverde, stretching on for days, sometimes weeks, dry and hot and lonely. He'd sit in the shade and think about his book, the new one with the murder mystery (the killer was the new ranch hand everyone liked so much, but he worried readers knew that secret too soon). Now and then he'd catch a glimpse of her through the post office window. She spoke for a long time to Mrs. Winnie, who owned the sandwich shop and pizzeria over by the highway, the closest thing to a restaurant within seven or eight miles. She'd mail letters for Clyde Bueller to his son in the state prison. Sometimes an unfamiliar car would skid into the dirt lot and a young man in a suit would run inside with a stack of packages, then leave as soon as he could, racing back to work.

But usually the afternoons were quiet. The three rural route mail carriers wouldn't return until five, when Molly would lock the front door and disappear into the back with old Beverly Craddock, the other clerk. Half an hour later, Molly would walk across the street and she'd find John either back to work on edits or writing letters at the kitchen table, but often he'd have dinner well under way. Maybe even finished. She'd shower and change and help with final touches. Back porch dinners. Flowers and wind chimes. Then they'd retire to their books.

It all started with the books. Not long after they first waved to one another all those years ago, he had to mail a short stack of signed copies to friends (acquaintances really) who wrote for magazines or newspapers, or friends who wanted signed copies. She applied posted and went about her business. When he returned the next day with more, she asked about them, the small stacks of bundles going out.

"Anything to do with those big boxes we dropped off at your place last week?"

"They're books. My new book, actually."

She'd nod and weigh the next parcel, and the next, setting them aside all stamped and measured. He expected her to ask about the book, but she didn't. He wasn't disappointed, but he was certainly more curious about her as she rang up the last one and handed him his receipt with a knowing smile, then placed the outgoing packages into a large canvas cart. She disappeared into the back, and he went home.

The next day he mailed books to those who were only vaguely interested, and the next day to people he barely knew, distant family members, former coworkers and students. Anybody. Any chance to nod hello, ask about her day, and then wave again from afar, smiling as she'd wave back. On Friday afternoon, just before five, he brought one for her.

"I thought you might be interested."

"I might," she said.

"Let me know what you think?" he almost said.

"I will," her eyes replied.

A week later, Delores at the library whispered that Molly Wren had been in asking about his other books. She checked out his first one. Two weeks later she borrowed the second. Delores always whispered these developments even though they were alone in the library on a quiet Bulverde afternoon.

On another such afternoon, just after five p.m., Molly appeared on his doorstep. She wore her post office uniform and carried three books for him to sign, the one he gave her and two new copies of his first two novels. She caught him off guard in his old writing robe and he felt his face blush with fire, but he still offered her iced tea. They sat on the porch swing and he asked her about her favorite authors. He asked her about the poetry she wrote in college. He asked about her pen pals in middle school. He asked about her travels. He asked what she thought of the coyotes singing in the hills as the highway lights twinkled through the sweeping darkness beyond Bulverde at night. He asked about her feelings about salsa verde enchiladas, and would she like to go with him, just a short drive into town (which is what everyone in Bulverde called San Antonio). They spoke long into the evenings that followed, and the evenings that followed, going on twenty years.

They spoke excitedly about new books and old books. They whispered quietly on politics and giggled in the dark of their bed about the things they overheard at the fire station BBQ. They worried over bills, cried about George Floyd, and they distrusted each other only twice, each of them sleepless after tense evenings when neither of them had any true reason to fret. It took them a few days to understand as much, to finally speak openly and find relief in one another. They soon continued with their back porch dinners and small waves from the front porch swing through the post office window.

He bought her flowers on Thursdays and made them BLTs on Mondays. She picked up pizza some Fridays and left him morning poems by the percolator. Not much changed in Bulverde in twenty years and they didn't think much would as they spoke about the future together in bed. But there was only one way to find out, and he said as much in a small letter he wrote her to tell her how much he loved her, and to ask her what she thought if he made the ranch hand a decoy in his murder mystery (the killer was *really* the doctor from town, driven by jealousy). He sealed the envelope and walked it to the post office, sliding it through the slot beside the door where old Beverly Craddock would find it and hand it to Molly soon enough.

Then John walked back to the porch swing where he sat with iced tea (it was too hot for coffee now, even for him) and waited for five o'clock and for everything Molly might have to say when she came home.

James

they say he owned a gas station
out in the west Texas hill country
and as he grew old and his kids all
moved away, wife gone, the other
men in town would take advantage
of his kindness and loneliness by
asking for credit, by asking for gas,
by visiting his shack on the edge
of town, swamp cooler in the big
front window, and they'd say, "Hey
Jimmy, get us some beer, we're all
broke!" and he'd go get them beer
and they'd send him time and time
again until my grandfather showed
up and said, "Dad, they're taking
advantage of you!"—my grandaddy
moved his father back home to San
Antonio, where he got to see my father
and one day me, all four of us carrying
the same name, and in some ways,
the same burden: burdens of kindness
made heavy by the duplicitous in
this world, and in the end, loneliness
made stark by the miles between us
and the years skittering away like
sand across a gas station lot in the
west Texas wind, night falling hard
and the moon up there so still and
quiet on another Friday night alone

Quatrains for Sagebrush Lane

dawn fades up into realization like a
specter from the past who feels its
revenge drawing near, and I wait for
it to find me, to end our shared regret

across the room the grandfather clock
stares unmoving, the human construct
of time lost to silence and deprivation
as the trees outside reach for the sun

the chain-link fence gate stands ajar
as small thumb-sized leaves tumble
across my father's dead lawn—now
I sense the truest meaning of time

I can hear the highways cutting through
the neighborhood like scars that cannot
fully heal, whispering their promise of
some other place waiting for us tonight

Quiescent

cool air fills the space
between the bedroom down
the hall and the living room
chair where my father sat late
into evenings, air soft and silent
in the conditioned calm
of those south Texas nights; I'd
write and stare out the window
at the gnarled oak trees and the cats
and squirrels who would play there,
and then rise and traverse that span
to his chair where we'd talk in the
glow of his television, the fan above
slowly spinning and the lights
dimmed to a blue yawn shaped
by late night talk shows, sometimes
basketball, sometimes the news,
maybe a black and white film, and then
I'd look up and see him drifting back into sleep so
I'd return to the keyboard and the lamp-lit darkness
of the bedroom to type some more and wonder
where all this silent static might lead us

we're both still at it, thousands of miles apart tonight,
he in his chair in the cool, calm air of his San Antonio
nights, and me with my keyboard and lamp
wherever this is, always wanting to traverse
that distance between us to see his face look up
and smile, to sit beside him and feel the night hush

I feel it still, age beyond age, night beyond night,
a gravitational pull that will last long after we are both
gone to another calm, cool realm of light and silence

Is this the place?

is this the place?
the sun and the
howling floods?
is this all there is?

this underpass by the university?
will we come here to rest in the
night? in the great collective wail
and raise our hands to the sky,
asking why? begging not the end?

is this continual parch sustainable,
regrettable, foreseeable, excusable?
are these waters coming down a
punishment we deserve or a gift
from a god who sleeps through every
alarm bell only to roll over in the
night and crush its young, unwitting?

is there nothing in the air but saturated
clouds and when they pass nothing
but dust and wind and the cries of those
lost to the great tides coursing through the
underpass by the university, the great
sweeping away of you and me and the
reasons we kept for doing nothing to
stop this world from turning against us?

that's right

nothing in the air but our dust and our cries
        for help and salvation,
and the burning yellow
        indifference of the sun

Home
(Reprise)

he doesn't know where he'd like to stay for the rest of
existence, when his existence is no more

cremation solves so many problems but he doesn't
know if he'll need his body in the next life

they said he might and they said it might be a sin, but
they don't know for sure and will say so if cornered

he looks to the horizon and listens to the whispers and
the promises they can never keep

he watches the hands of the clock spin opposing one
another, time running out / adding up at the same pace

the weight of everything we have missed in each
other's lives over the many years is crushing

oh the nostalgic regret of impossibilities

I say I don't know what the next life holds, or if there
is a next life to sustain is, but one day we will find out

for now, I ask you (as I asked him):

spread my ashes in the waters of the Hudson River in
upstate New York, and spread some more in the waters
snaking through downtown San Antonio, and if there is
any of me left, let the waves in Corpus Christi take me
to sea

at that he quietly nodded and we listened
to the night fall down upon us

with all its infinite and unmatched power
silent and indifferent, despite the air's
sweet southern taste of home

Ineffable

we were outside the patio cantina
watching a line of rusted boxcars
lumber through the desert air beyond the reach
of the cantina's carnival lights
glinting among voices and memories and ghosts

in some ways I am still at that southside patio
drinking in your honor and in your debt,
drinking in neon and catatonic delight

toasting the things we don't speak of,
things we cannot let go,
no matter the hour
or how many boxcars declare their willingness
to carry that burden into the night

The Telephone Pole on Cherry St.

the telephone pole caught fire last Saturday with
the black ocean swale swinging low from the sky

they came racing through the storm, through the
threat of hail and rain, pointed their guns, fired

and doused the pole from the city tap sending a
thunderhead through the air snapping the wires

and knocking out windows from the rowhouse
across the alley, and someone will thank them

while others will watch, mute, then write angry
letters to the newspaper about the damage done

which someone might read and then throw away,
wondering about toothpaste, pot roast, a flat tire,

and how to feed their eleven starving children as
a new telephone pole goes up over on Cherry St.

Empty Spaces

Highway 410 is an irregular loop that, a generation or two ago, stood as the unofficial marker for the outer reaches of San Antonio. Until the city vastly outgrew it. Now 410 runs through the guts of the city, an inner loop of urban sprawl. Highway 1604 became the next marker, the outer loop, another circular highway on the furthest edges of the city, much of it running through vast, empty scrubland. Dried riverbeds of yellow stone. Clusters of low oaks looking like dead spiders. Trickling arroyos snaking through tall grass where trash and highway debris would catch and hold for generations.

From these points you could look toward downtown and see the lights and rolling hills of housing developments, shopping malls, and the nest of highways spiraling into infinity. But over time, the city outgrew that outer loop as well with endless apartment complexes and car dealerships, but for a while during my childhood and early twenties, San Antonio pulsated between the two. It was in that period when Jesse and I decided to drive the entirety of Loop 1604, just for the hell of it, which we assumed would take us most of the day.

But even with traffic involved, it only took us three hours, an underwhelming yet significant amount of time. In the same span we could have driven to the coast and relaxed on the beach, eaten fried shrimp, drank cold beer from a cooler. We could have driven to Houston, or most of the way to Dallas. We could have watched a movie at the downtown IMAX and snuck into the second half of another before going to the wax museum to laugh at the misshapen "Heroes of the Alamo" exhibit. Instead, we drove in a circle in his faded green Jetta with a missing passenger side-view mirror.

Jesse would chain smoke when we drove anywhere, especially long road trips. The curling tendrils of silver swayed and slipped through the cracked window, the old butts in the dashboard tray overflowing to the floor. We spoke of childhood memories and how we feared our fathers' hobbies would become our own, his father's being digital poker and bingo, my father's being golf, which I soon gave up but I was still fumbling through the local par-3 courses one at a time back then. When we finally completed the loop, neither of us felt much joy, only relief. What a foolish accomplishment, but an accomplishment nonetheless. When we took the next exit leading back into the city, Jesse noticed we were near the cemetery on the southwestern part of town where he had buried his mother years before.

He wanted to go visit and I had no objections. I hadn't paid my respects in the ten years since it happened. We were in high school at the time, right near graduation. I remembered her fondly, her kind smile and watchful concern as we grew with increasing abandon. She would drive us for Chinese buffet lunches together then drop us off at the mall so he and I could watch American releases of dubbed Jackie Chan movies. For some we were the only two people in the theater. We grew less innocent over time. In our later teens we stole liquor, acquired fake IDs, ran around with girls from other schools late into the night. Despite her best Christian efforts, we navigated those years in such a way as to live outside of the Lord's sight and by consequence outside of His love. Or so we thought. Maybe she knew something about unending love that we didn't. Maybe none of us knew anything. But she was kind, and in this world that's a rare enough grace to make her a saint. What could possibly fill the gap she left in his world?

We drove to the corner of the cemetery where he remembered burying her, and we found the right tree that marked the row where we'd find her headstone. But it wasn't there. We tried the next row. And the next. We split up and worked over half the cemetery before Jesse called his sister to confirm. No, we were right. Go back the tree, head toward the distant highway just visible through the squat line of oaks, the eighteenth grave. But the spot for the eighteenth grave was just a wide gap between Cynthia Morales (1961 – 1999) and Ricardo Herrera (1938 – 1998). Where was she?

The space didn't seem wide enough for a missing grave, but it was certainly not the same spacing as others. After I listened to him call other family members for confirmation, and receiving none, I went and sat in the passenger seat with one foot out of the open car door. Cicadas chittered and whined all around in the late afternoon heat, smothering bloated waves of dense air wading through the cemetery. I watched him pace in circles and I thought about his mother, remembering when she tried to get me to read the *Left Behind* book series, saying, "It's just like Stephen King. You liked *The Stand*, right? You'll love this." It wasn't like *The Stand* and I knew it before the first page, but I read it on their couch until she went to bed just to be kind.

"Well, they never bought her a headstone," Jesse said when he came back to the car. "And everyone thinks she was buried in a different part of the cemetery, but at least we have the right cemetery."

"Do we?" I asked.

He stared through the windshield for a moment, then shrugged. "Who knows."

Jesse started the car and said he'd figure it out. I knew he would, but the impact of the discovery (or lack of) hit him with too much force to deal with it in that moment. He asked if I wanted to go to Baker Street for the night, our usual bar over on the northwest side in the Medical District. He liked it there because sometimes nurses stopped in. I told him we'd find her, get that headstone. We were broke but I had a feeling we'd find a way, somehow. Jesse just nodded. When we arrived, the uneven parking lot out front was almost empty, the neon lights in the blacked-out windows matching the magenta and purple swath of sky plastered over the western horizon. We went in and found our usual seats at the bar. Every other stool stood empty.

We ordered. Jesse lit another cigarette as a bartender we didn't recognize set down our jack & coke doubles. We drank them in silence. On the TV, the Spurs were losing to the Knicks by a dozen. But it was only the third quarter.

I nodded to the TV and said, "Lot of time left."

Jesse exhaled a long plume of silver. "That's what they always say."

Transmissions from Beyond

the ghosts in this house have gone silent
and I wait in the bathtub with $4 wine,
a book, and all the hot water I can stand
until the small hours shift into darkness

the hue of dusk in San Antonio comes in
subtle waves of rose and dust, plum and
black felt lining a coffin closing just a
little more, just a hint, one faint whisper

from this bathtub I could be anywhere
and it could be any time, it doesn't have
to be an hour before old friends and bar
friends leave their homes for neon fire

but it *is* that time, and I rise and dry and
step into the hallway of my father's home
and I listen;
                two days before, the voices came
again, a conversation in hushed tones
like a radio play, transmissions from beyond,
but   this time
                        no one shook my
shoulder as I napped through another
unemployed afternoon of heavy sunlight
and shadows here in this house, my rock
against the waves

the highways of San Antonio twist and
sweep into long curves into the sky, a
place now humming orange against the
starless night, blotted out by fast food signs,
street lights, the halogen lamp hanging
from a wooden pole in the cracked lot

outside Baker Street Pub where I walk
in and find a stool beside the universe

the idea of voices and sounds and time
cascade in a dream wash through these
rooms and human spaces; a howl of
laughter in the same air 6 hours later

means nothing, the jukebox buddha-patient
in the corner there beside the specials sign
and the dart machines where, 6 hours prior,
Jesse looks me in the eye and throws a dart,

a bullseye without even looking,
the nightly hustle complete, betting
with college kids about who will buy
drinks next, and we never go home sober

it's a miracle shot but it's already gone,
and someday someone will be sweeping
the floor across the bar and the dart
machine will play its little song, and

they'll think, why did it do that?
how many years have I swept away?
how much neon can whiskey absorb?
how much whiskey will make this all
fade to nothing?

I am embarrassed by the hours I
spent sitting on a stool inebriated
yet I want nothing more than to
feel that tilt-a-whirl happiness again

the clack of pool tables racked,
damp rings on wooden bar tops,

conversations like a radio play;
transmissions // from // beyond

that's all that's left, those waves
we've made by our movement in
circles, bathtub highway bar to bar
to another lonely bar in search of

…god I don't even know what, chasing
ghosts and hopes and wonderments
maybe love, certainly lust and radiant
eyes across a dark crowded room

holding those eyes, that look, a second more,
speaking hushed into ears while laughter and
music erupts all around and then you both
lean in and kiss and smile and open your eyes

to the dust of the universe

an empty room in another state

go fill the tub, as hot as you can get it

and later on, if you're able

leave something wild for the ghosts who come next

I Want the Simplest Things for This World

the bomb-crater soul of this world is failing,
the smoke and the fire and the heart-dust
filtering through fingers like so much ash, and
when I hear someone in line ahead of me say
such simple refrains as *yes please* and *thank you*
I almost want to cry that these dumb platitudes
will never be enough to drag us beyond
the high tide mark—and its coming, the cruel
desperations are coming, the boots and the guns
and the crosses on fire in your neighbor's yard,
and I just want to hold you in the warm Texas
sun and show you all the love this hardscrabble
land has never given us,
but I fear none of us will ever
have the chance to speak our hearts,
that all the children running through the fields
of rye we all read about as children will never
stand a chance against the fire and the smoke
blotting out the blue skies I search for every single
time I open my eyes and think of home

but I'll try, even if all I have are the simplest
of wishes for this world on fire, I'll try

Nefarious

yellow-red hues
of Texas highway afternoons
running hot into August
with the car radio
blasting Spoon and the windows
rolled down all the way
to the bar we all called home

we'd put five in the jukebox
and give five more to the old man selling tacos
bar to bar out of a carry-cooler,
and everyone else did the same; cigarette girls
would come through and scan your ID
and give you two free packs,
whiskey girls giving out t-shirts and
the music would drown out
the electric dart games and the TVs and we'd eat
those tacos and wait
to hear our songs come up and the night
never turned to day, never broke against the rocks of
dawn

it stayed that way
like a tombstone, every date
and name etched forever

walking in ten years later, it felt like that,
like visiting your own grave

we were the last ones standing: no kids, wife, house,
we were criminals of a kinder variety,
always something to grin about,
and enough cash left for one
more drink before the next grift rose up into sight,

into the bloodstream of hot nights and neon
spilling across that Texas horizon and
resting us easy into our summer graves nefarious

dark of the outskirts

San Antonio, can you call to me with any
sweeter vision than this distant horizon?
humming purple and scarlet, reflecting
the setting sun behind me as I limp home
from the west, front right tire in the back
seat and the car leaning low into the slow
groove of the donut, 40 mph along the far
right lane, letting big rigs pass by as I inch
closer and closer to the end of my night

I dream of Alpine heights and galaxies unfolding
I dream of cavalry posts abandoned to legend
I dream of hill country cemeteries abandoned
I dream of Marfa lights flitting into the sky

full night now, stars melting away into the distant
hum of the city, standing on the side of the road
to rest, to rub my eyes, listen to the freight trucks
scream past before sinking into the soft sea of
the Texas breeze running through guajillo trees
and burrograss, delicate larkspur, cacti like Picasso
paintings in the soft yellow of my headlights,
and with no trucks this becomes a peaceful place,
making me sad now that my tire blew out before
I ever made it to Big Bend, Fort Davis, to beautiful
Alpine again, to relive a childhood wonder, instead I
am in the dark of the outskirts, moonstruck alone

I dream of white alkali flats and golden sand eternal
I dream of railroads rusted to skeletal connotations
I dream of observatories watching dead stars burn
I dream and dream and cannot stop dreaming

I'm close enough now I pick up San Antonio radio

stations and the speed limit drops back down to 75
but I'm still rolling along at 35, 40, 45 when daring,
the unfamiliar limp and hum of my old Nissan on
the last journey we'll ever make, having crossed this
great land once and twice again like encore comets,
and now we roll slow, taking in every blinking radio
tower, the soft glowing windows of distant ranches,
and when I return I might speak of failure but in truth
I reinforced the dream of my youth, kept it sacred,
saving it for some future self-revelation, but until then
the lights of San Antonio and the windows down, the
radio up, the cry of big rigs carry my through the
final miles until I see my father's mailbox and ease
into the safe harbors of home for one more sacred night

even the immortals know

the cat next door is caught on the roof again
he calls through the shade of
the night, his voice wavering languorous
like the sway of the bedroom
window curtain—black and torpid
in the sweltering South Texas heat

the cat, he gets caught up there 3 or sometimes 4
times per week, and he always seems to find
his way down when nobody is around, just finds
his way up to caterwaul in misery,
and the next thing you know,
he's gone, like some
great-grandson of Macavity,
no explanation needed,
no midnight theatrics denied

in the morning, he waits down the street beneath
the lilac trees for the butterflies to dance,
a saint of the suburban sadness infecting not
just this city, but every city, every small town
and possible lifetime that awaits each of us
down any given street, any given choice we make
the lord of these possibilities waits in the lilac
trees for the sun to rise and fall so he may climb
the branches of the young oak and sing his woesome
song of long dead love, of six, seven, eight lives
ill-spent and lost to the whims of the world,
the weight of it all settling over this room,
this bed, this heart, this hope, this madness

and when the sun goes down and Macavity goes up
the curtain will ruffle in the same old wind,
curling against the chair where the wine waits,

where jackets / shoes reside after bar-hopping all night, and when he calls out there is a moment when the earth seems to pause and even the immortals know the pain it is to be a living, breathing thing

                                                        alone

Sanctuary

there is a small hill near
my father's home in
San Antonio where a single
lamppost spreads a golden circle
into the night just catching
all four corners of the silent
residential intersection, all homes
dark, all streets empty, palms
and salt grass cutting jagged edges
into the midnight reminding
me of same such quiet walks in
Los Angeles towns in outlying
hills, of the sunsets in San Francisco
too, and sometimes writer friends
would quote Kerouac
and his California dispatches, but
when words speed-trip
through the midnight filter
I am there on that small hill
with the orange dome over the far
downtown San Antonio skyline
matching my lamppost
sanctuary, a breeze that comes
and dies with a cat watching
from the darkened alley
where someone placed his or her
black plastic garbage bins inordinate
and askew, then car headlights lead
to footsteps and the city fades
as beneath the wild oak canopy the
dark of life takes hold again
and sends me home with whispers
to share with no one at all, or
maybe they were waiting

for you all this time to create a
dead city jazz for you and I

Mama & Papa

Hemingway's Poolhall on Wurzbach Avenue became a regular haunt in my final days in San Antonio, but I never expected to meet the man himself in that nefarious establishment. His reputation solidified into a thunderhead force within minutes of his arrival. Every time he shoved someone out of the way to get another beer, his buddies laughed and egged him on as he mugged and posed and talked in a loud, clean baritone about the men he'd seen die in Spain and Africa and how he'd outlasted them all. He shouted "Bully!" whenever someone played Foreigner or Bad Company on the jukebox. The little song the electric dart machine chirped out from the corner every five minutes made him roar with delight and he'd sing back in imitation. His beard and teeth glowed blue in the neon of the bar.

Hemingway was king shit on a Thursday night until Mama Fratelli hustled through the door. The crowd parted for her as she prowled her way to the bar, her meaty arms crossing as she leaned forward and called for three fingers of Evan Williams. Hemingway noticed and called out for four fingers of the same, and he ordered the bartender to "make those fingers all thumbs." He laughed at himself in an echo of sycophantic applause.

Mama Fratelli adjusted her black beret, spat on the ground, and slugged the glass back before slamming it on the counter. People nearby nudged me to watch Hemingway, and he did the same, finishing with a theatrical, lip-smacking *AHHHH* as he slammed his glass down.

Mama Fratelli glared at Hemingway and told him to piss off. She said she'd just dealt with a bunch of asshole kids and had spent the afternoon drowning them one by one in some goddamn pirate's cove, or some such nonsense, and she didn't have time for another little boy's antics. She was always saying crazy things like this, and we avoided her for the most part, but today we all leaned forward to watch and listen.

"Mama," Papa said, "I do believe you'd make a son out of me. After all, you have a face only a son could love."

Silence struck the bar, and after a long beat the dart machine chirped its little song. Hemingway chuckled, a low assured thing, but I got the feeling somehow that he didn't like how quiet it got.

Mama Fratelli squinted at Hemingway and then at the bartender, who rushed to refill her glass. She slugged it back, pointed to a table in the rear, and flexed her arm, saying, "Over the top—one go. And when we're done you pack up your little boy scout troop and get the hell out of my bar."

"*Your* bar?!" Hemingway charged forward with such force he knocked over three stools. The crowd parted and the two hulking forces of nature stomped their way through the bar to the table. We swiftly gathered around. Hemingway threw himself into a chair and began rolling up his khaki shirt sleeve as Mama Fratelli spun her chair backwards and dumped herself down, her elbow hitting the table, ready to go.

"God damn," Hank the old postal carrier said. "Fifty bucks on the old man."

That started a flurry of bets. Tom Waits tipped back his pork pie hat and began collecting, shouting figures and names, licking a pencil he pulled from behind his ear and scribbling each in a notepad. Yeah yeah, he heard Hunter Thompson call out for a tenner on Papa. And yeah yeah, he heard Sam Shepard call out for a sawbuck on Mama. So did Plath, Bradbury, and even McCullers, who then doubled it because, as she cackled over her Southern Comfort, "Bad bitches stick together."

That got me thinking. I pulled on Tom's elbow and he narrowed his eyes at me.

"Ten grand on Mama Fratelli," I said.

"Christ, kid, you got that kind of bread just lying around in a place like this? Don't ask me to walk you out later, that's all I'm saying."

"Just gimme ten large on the lady."

"Uhhh, can you prove you're good for it?"

I pulled a stack of bills wrapped with a fresh band from my inner pocket, then tucked it back.

"Since when are you so hog high? You ain't gonna ask me to help ya bury nobody, are ya?"

"Look, am I good for it or what?"

"I'll sing at your funeral if it makes you feel better," he muttered, writing it down, then he shouted, "Ten large for Jimmy. Done and done. All bets are closed!"

It was time to start. Tom began giving both contestants an introduction before Hemingway bellowed "Stuff it, skinny," and then Mama and Papa gripped their hamfists in a meaty slap.

Papa said *on three*. Mama said *two*. He said *one*.

They heaved into each other, straining, sweat beading on their foreheads. The crowd roared, shouted, pleaded, clapped, howled, and stamped their feet in manic rage and desire as both arms wavered upright, barely moving for almost a full minute until Hemingway's brawny forearm, though it bulged and strained, fell inch by inch as Mama Fratelli stared into his eyes, boring a hole right through him. And then— BAM—his arm bounced off the table in defeat.

The crowd erupted with laughter and jeers, but through the din I heard Mama tell Hemingway to get the hell out. She tossed the chair aside and disappeared through the ravenous mob. I pushed my way through to the back, looking for Tom to collect, and I found him jiggering an Addams Family pinball machine. When I asked him for my winnings, he smirked at me sideways and said, "Ahhh, jeez, kid, ya really want to call that in now? In front of God and everyone?"

He damn well knew I did, so he relented and exhaled a ring of cigarette smoke as we left the pinball machine flashing and ringing behind us, begging us to return. The back hall led us past reeking bathrooms then turned right and right again before the stairwell down, where through a door Tom greeted Ernest Borgnine playing solitaire at an old steel desk that looked like something someone had hauled out of a Navy destroyer circa Iwo Jima.

"What's this? You ain't supposed to bring anyone down here," Borgnine said, indignant to the world.

"Kid won twenty thou-shekels when Mama went over the top."

"Over the top? On who?"

"That beefy elephant gun who broke the toilet on nickel-shot night."

"Hemingway? That asshole? Jeez, if someone woulda said something I woulda got in on the action. Nobody tells me nothing!" Borgnine stood and turned, producing a key from his pocket, and opening a safe behind him. "Twenty grand on a bet. Fella can make a nice living that way."

Borgnine handed me four stacks of cash, loosely wrapped but it was all there.

"Now beat it, kid," Tom said. "You're making me nervous standing there counting it like some sorta bank clerk high on his own product."

I thanked them both but Borgnine was already asking for details and Tom was lighting up a stogie so I closed the door behind me and made my way upstairs.

I almost went to go buy a round, but I thought about what Tom said earlier, about walking out of there with all that dough, so when I got to the top I opened the back service door and slipped into the broken night, shards of moon falling through dead palm trees and telephone wires. I kept a close watch over my shoulder the whole way home, a long walk through apartment complex mazes and back streets. When I got there I saw Cruz was still awake, rolling his week's worth of cigarettes in the dim glow of a kitchen lamp.

"You okay?" he asked, a cigarette stuck in the corner of his mouth. "You look like you've seen a ghost."

"I have," I said, slapping the money down on the table, all four bundles. "A whole bunch of dead presidents."

He leaned back, staring at the pile. "You're not going to ask me to help you bury someone, are you?"

"No."

"Are you going to ask me to help you spend this?"

"I just might."

He exhaled a ring of smoke and laughed to himself. "I always knew one of us would ride the other's coattails into the sunset. I just didn't think it would happen on a Thursday."

"Let's get the hell out of this town, once and for all. You in?"

"No, I'm out, already gone, way past the horizon," he said, reaching for the money, cradling it with a smile, "and you better go pack your bags and catch up or you might never see us again."

So that's exactly what I did.

Jazz Annex

Gil hits the memory machine //
fifty cents a song, then
strolls 'cross the room toward the lit cigarette, and
—the maw is open—
Jesse lights another smoke
brings the gray horizon down level
with the eyes and he talks of all the wonders
from the seven corners of the world as he
himself anchors the corner stool, sidled up
to a woman twice his age and just his lifestyle—
—Gil now is behind the bar, reaching
for a bottle of our whiskey, shooed away
by Jackie the blonde of jazz and she is smoking herself
as Gil hits the memory machine once more //
coins falling between floorboards,
strolls 'cross the room to his girl, and there are other
girls and guys of all types
traipsing through from one bar to the next, all the
bars in a row where pool cues clutter and music
drifts down through eternal back alleys to
the Annex where jazz and Jackie
and Brian sit with Gil, Jesse lighting a smoke,
whole groups of sweet talkers jumping against the
floorboards to stay
warm in the night, hoping not to go cold after 2 a.m.
when the doors close and the register dies
and the smoke floats up past our coffins to the moon
up there waiting to inhale our love—
and Gil is home now with his girl, quiet and maybe
in some sort of temporary peace, much unlike
Jesse smoking still in darkened rooms with me,
and Jackie is gone now, Brian too, just ghosts down
the street like all nighthawks,
little manifestations

of the darkness moving within the dark,
looking back, looking forward, gone gone gone

Transience

Stray and I talked about walking from New York City
to San Francisco and I always worried he or I would kill
ourselves before we had the chance, but then jobs and
money started coming in again and those long walks
along farm roads faded from our vision, the nights under
train bridges sinking to black, the crickets and little
crinkle of fire deafening in our ears as subways and
traffic held us in place in our lives of new jobs, new
homes, new futures, and maybe it was for the best that
we didn't...
but
Stray, old friend, I wish
we tried—the fact that you even asked
was joy enough for one wayward lifetime,
and I thank you

Ingram Park Mall

sunstroke implosion of commercial incandescence
where we found arcades to plunder and sneakers
that pumped up to our exact tween specifications,
Sam Goody cassettes of Selena Quintanilla, Huey
Louis and the News, the first blue Weezer album,
as grandparents walked circuitous routes along
each arm of the mall, meeting in the central food
court for Chinese, pizza, Chick-fil-a, whatever we
wanted so long as neon signage hummed overhead
and cool air billowed to make us forget it was over
100 degrees outside, even hotter in the parking lot,
that moat of molten asphalt where minivans and
lowriders roamed and anchored themselves, waiting
for us, those 80s kids, 90s kids, children of capitalism
with cash to spare and time to kill in movie theaters,
comic shops, never thinking such places could fade
to empty halls of commerce, echoey canyons where
our grandparents no longer exist, where Salena is but
a memory, where arcade consoles sit blank and silent,
and the rest of us who made it out of the Ingram Park
Mall parking lot are now buried under the weight of
environmental decay, medical bills, insurrectionist
propaganda, war, and a morning commute that never
seems to end—but it will, as all things do in time

The Magician

love will come and go, he says,
but the aching fever in between
is forever

I sense he's deep into the gin again
as he sends transmissions
from his plantation house
cradled by heat and ancient lore, explaining
how art and communication
can be mutually exclusive; the act is the thing,
   —he says, the good will die, the bad may yet live,
heaven will rage as the fires of hell dance,
and in the confusion, he says, is when you play your
trick,
    make your magic,
show the world your slight of hand,
and then slip behind the silk curtain just in time

love will come and go, come and go,
but this fever dream in between is forever,
he cries out, roving the empty rooms
of his sprawling, crumbling southern manse
begging the old gods of the southern plains
for peace and love and recompense—in vain

years later, I hear his echoes still,
the laughter, the crying,
—and in my ignorance, I don't know
if I believe him just yet, but
the best magicians never reveal their final trick

Two Burnt Matches

I stood on the corner of the town square
in Mason, TX near the small veterans
memorial and watched
as the cars turned the corner
and sailed around the square,
disappearing beyond,
the closed one-screen movie house
the closed five & dime
the small remnants of what
used to be my family's
hometown

I had three matches and three cigars
in my pocket but didn't like the odds, so
I crossed the square and walked inside
the only café open on Sunday

no free tables, but the waitress
set me up at the small bar with a
fork, spoon, knife
all rolled into a white
cloth napkin

for a long time nobody bothered
to come take my order,
but that was fine by me
I had come to find
my great-grandfather's grave
and had failed, and now
I sat and watched the town eat, all of them
coming from farms and trailers and little ramshackle
cottages just beyond the town square
all of them eating and talking about a million
things that people who lived

here talked about, simple things
beautiful in their natural blandness
like wind against
cornstalks in the evening

finally, I ate a chicken fried
steak that was almost as big
and thick than my plate
and watched as others ate
pecan pie, chocolate pudding
and biscuits smothered
in butter and honey

the waitress who set me up asked
where I came from, and we talked a bit
about the town
about her son in the Army
about my journey
about the fact that the town
had three cemeteries: the new one,
the one I walked through, and
another old one three miles
due east, and that I might have more
luck there, and to come back
on a Saturday

because everything is open on Saturday
and the pecan pie would be half off

I said I would, and meant it
then left the café, walking down
past the one-screen movie house
that showed one movie per night
at 7 p.m., but not on Sundays

I found my car and considered

the long drive back to San Antonio
through endless hill country arroyo and sage
and one part of me started that
long drive home, while the other burned
through two matches
to light one cigar
and began walking due east
along the gravel shoulder and into
into the coming
dusk
to find that last cemetery
before nightfall

part of me never seeing Mason again
and part of me still walking that
gravel shoulder, searching for a stone
to call my own

Lighthouse

he was an oracle somehow, because when he came back
from work where he taught blind people to use
computers, he handed me a print-out of a story that one
of the blind students wrote using a keyboard, and while
I don't recall the story—it was about a dog, that's all I
can remember—he seemed to know I was the only one
at home who would understand why it meant something,
twelve years old with my grandfather, silent and
knowing, humble and stoic, reclining in his chair and
reading the newspaper as the television played out the
day and I laid down on the couch to read that story
beside him, and I think he knew, he had to know, that
smile he gave me when I finished the story and told him
why I liked it; of course he understood the tides and
coastlines of my lifespan, it explains every little thing

Dreamcatchers

the southern breeze spun the wind chimes
and dreamcatchers beneath my grandparents'
enclosed back porch where they'd sit on hot
afternoons or in the violet evenings with the
bug zapper glowing blue, palms and plants

and the bbq grill radiating heat, cigarettes and
cans of soda, love, gentle laughter, thick grass
that sponged beneath our feet, the sky above
their home remains to me an ageless wonder,
as does my memory of my grandmother's smile,

also the creak of her back door going in, the cool air-
conditioning, and I want to go back there and tell her
how things will turn out after these things are gone,
but I can't imagine it's all gone for good; it still exists:

my grandfather rustling in the garage for something,
the sound of laundry rattling, cool cans of soda
in our hands with chilled condensation dribbling
down the sides, pastel sheets on the guest room bed
and dreamcatchers overhead as the lights go out,

but there's always one more tip-toe to the fridge
through TV glow laughter and soft worn carpets,
then lights out for good, everyone in bed all cool
and dark until one day tomorrow doesn't come for

anyone

Dominion

From the trailer's front porch, if you looked all the way down the gravel cul-de-sac, you could see the iron gates of the Dominion. If you took three steps into the yard of dead crabgrass you could see the guard booth beside the gate. And if you walked into the middle of the rounded heart of the cul-de-sac, even Magnolia could see the first few mansions peeking over the edge of the hills beyond. Cars came and went from the gate a few times an hour. Sometimes a Land Rover. Sometimes a sports car with some Italian name she couldn't pronounce. Sometimes even a limousine. But the only cars that came down her quiet street were old Hondas or pickup trucks with rusted bumpers, like her father's. He'd been gone all day again and she'd grown bored of daytime TV, so Magnolia walked down the cul-de-sac to see if she could spot herself a fancy car or celebrity.

"Nine years old is old enough to take care of yerself," her father often said, usually on his way out to the Silver Fox, a little cinderblock saloon with no windows and a trough out back men used as a urinal. It was only a five-minute walk but he always drove, "just in case," he said. In case of what she couldn't imagine. But he went almost every day, and when school was out for the summer she'd sit around and grow bored all alone in the small row of trailers along the edge of the Dominion, the wealthiest neighborhood in Texas south of Austin and west of Houston, side by side with one of the poorest.

Magnolia stood on the corner across from the guard booth and waited in the afternoon heat, a sweltering blanket sort of heat, heavy on the shoulders and forehead, hard to inhale. The kind of heat that made the distant end of her street shimmer in and out of focus. She watched the booth and wondered if anyone really sat behind the darkened windows, because when a car finally did arrive (nothing fancy, just a big SUV), the gate rolled out of the way all by itself, then shut with a definitive *cla-chunk*, then silence again.

People always talked about who lived in the Dominion, a big hobby among those in the trailers and shacks. There was the country singer her mom used to love, the stodgy old actor in those *Men in Black* movies, oilmen, cattlemen, the pastor of a local megachurch, famous athletes. She once overheard her daddy and his cousin Keith talk about some basketball player for the Spurs, "the little French kid," who owned a mansion that had a whole waterpark in this backyard. Slides and pools and even a lazy river, and the best part was that halfway along the river there was a snack bar and the basketball player and all his friends could get nachos and beer and all kinds of food and drinks and they'd just bob along and eat nachos under the shade of the trees guarding the river from the sun. It sounded like heaven to Magnolia.

She stood across from the gate, the cul-de-sac behind her. To her right, if she walked a little ways she'd cross a couple more streets with trailers and eventually the Silver Fox saloon near the main road. To her left, the road wound up into the hills, edging along the Dominion's fence. She knew it was a dead end up thataway so she never went up there too often. It was higher ground though and she wondered if it might give her a better view of the mansions beyond. So that's where she headed.

The paved road curved up past a couple nicer homes than her trailer court. They weren't as nice as those in the Dominion though, barely visible through the iron bars of the fence beyond the brush and brambles, past the yellow boulders and squat oaks and junipers baking in the afternoon sun. When she reached the end of the road, she found a half-constructed home, the ground dug up raw, a slab of cement waiting for the bones and innards to come next. Nearby a big yellow backhoe with its tank-like treads sat abandoned. She tried to climb on top to get a better view but the hot metal scorched her hands, so she wandered the abandoned construction site, kicking an old beer can she found, meandering along the property line until a little footpath appeared, leading through tufts of salt grass and wild rye. Magnolia followed it into the wasteland beyond.

The trail sloped down a little but she saw it ascended further up through the forest of dense trees, breaking free again into an open hilltop. She kept going, hoping for better views. The path became vague but she kept going, knowing enough to keep an eye out for scorpions and rattlesnakes and to avoid the tall grass to evade ticks. Even so, she'd be sure to check later and pluck them off with tweezers like her momma once showed her. Whenever the trees and brush cleared enough for her to get a better view beyond the fence, she always spotted another clearing ahead, a little closer to the Dominion, a little higher, and so she kept on walking, sweating in the sun and shielding her eyes whenever she broke free of the oaks.

Then a big house came into view, far closer than she expected it to be, just on the next hill. She didn't see the iron fence anymore. The house looked three stories tall with big balconies on each floor, and on each of those balconies she saw pools that flowed down into each other like a series of waterfalls. Was this the house with the waterpark? She didn't see any slides or lazy river. The only thing that stopped her from getting a better look was a sloping ravine, dense with greenery and brush, so she decided to work her way closer. What was the harm?

Magnolia weaved through tall, prickly plumes of agarito and hackberry, stumbling a bit as the ground sloped downward, jagged rocks clawing through the dead brambles. Her foot slipped again and she stumbled headlong through the brush, running to stay upright until she finally fell into a pile of scattered debris someone had thrown into the ravine. Boards and scrap wood caught her legs and she felt head first into the ground. Dazed for a moment, her vision swimming, but as she sat up she felt a throbbing, stabbing sensation on the bottom of her foot. Looking down she saw an old board flat against the bottom of her shoe. Something sharp had pierced the sole of her sneaker and when she yanked the board away, she screamed as the pain lanced through her foot. There was a rusty nail sticking out of the board about as long as her daddy's pointer finger, slightly bent and glistening with fresh, crimson blood.

Now her foot pulsed as if it had a heart of its own. The world still swam as she climbed up onto one foot and hopped away from the scattered debris, but she kept losing her balance. Magnolia leaned against a tree, seething with pain. She touched her head and felt the sensitive lump along her hairline. Her mind spun, unsure of what to do or even which way she'd come tumbling down the ravine. She couldn't see the house anymore. She couldn't see anything. But she knew she couldn't stay there sobbing. She needed help.

It took her an hour to find to the top of the ravine again, following the overgrown gulley until she found a way up, hopping from jagged boulder to boulder on one foot. Every time she landed on her bad foot she felt a jolt of pain and the squish of her bloody sock inside the shoe. When she reached the top, panting and sweating in the sun, the temp swelling well over a hundred by this point, she realized she still couldn't see the house with the little waterfalls no matter which way she turned. Nor the fence. She didn't panic though. It hadn't been that long of a walk from the construction site, maybe fifteen minutes, right? Maybe a little longer? Didn't matter. She couldn't be far. She kept walking.

And walking, limping really, favoring the punctured shoe, the foot soaking in blood, the throbbing pain that never seemed to lessen. She stopped a few times to rest her sore legs, looking for houses, for the fence, for the big yellow backhoe, but all she saw were more oak trees and scrubland. How could she have lost the way so easily? She walked on in the punishing heat. Her throat clicked, dry as the dirt pathways that seems to twist and go forever. Later, when she stopped to catch her breath, she noticed the sun sat lower in the sky than she expected. That made her more nervous than anything. She didn't want to be out in the hill country alone and bleeding with coyotes roaming at dusk. But then again, she'd be able to see the lights of home if it was dark out. She kept limping, trying to put thoughts of the night out of her mind.

By the time Magnolia found a house, the sun was touching the treeline. She knew she had been walking in the wrong direction for a long time but she worried that if she backtracked she'd get even more lost. So she kept going, her skin hot and her throat bone dry, feeling as dizzy as when she first fell. Then a rooftop came into sight. As she staggered through the last knots of brush into the yard, the back door opened and a woman wiping her hands with a rag called out to her, asking if something was wrong.

"My foot," Magnolia said, the last thing she remembered as she fell into the grass and fainted.

When she came back around, Magnolia smelled something baking—fresh bread?—and found herself on a couch inside what looked like a doctor's office, with boxes of gloves and bottles of pills on shelves, stethoscopes on hooks, and animal cages along the far wall beside an open door leading to what looked like a kitchen. The woman knelt before her, cleaning her foot with a warm wet cloth. Magnolia's shoe and sock lay on the floor, and it surprised her to see the sock wasn't soaked in blood, only stained in a small, neat circle. The woman, dressed in flannels and jeans, smiled at her and began applying an antibiotic cream.

"Don't worry, I'm just cleaning the wound. You have a puncture here that went all the way through. What was it?"

Magnolia told her about the rusty nail in the board and the stumble home. She began to apologize but the woman only shook her head and smiled.

"It's okay, it's okay," she woman said. "Drink that water there, just sips for now. You're extremely dehydrated and you have a nasty bump on your head. But thankfully you didn't bleed too much. Punctures rarely do unless you hit a good-sized artery or vein, and it looks like you got lucky."

"I thought I was bleeding a lot. I could feel it."

"Panic sweat. Humans sweat a lot through their feet, believe it or not. What I'm worried about now is your risk of infection, especially with rusty rails. Have you had your tetanus shot?"

Magnolia shook her head.

"You're sure?"

Magnolia hesitated.

"Can we call your parents and ask? Maybe they can meet us at urgent care."

"My dad isn't home. He goes to the Silver Fox."

"And your mom?"

Magnolia shook her head. The woman nodded, thinking it over, her shoulder-length hair bobbing as she finished wrapping the foot in white gauze. She knelt back and sighed.

"Well, you're going to need a doctor to look at this. I'm a veterinarian and it's clean enough for now but you need to make sure you're up on your shots or you need to get a booster. But you'll need your dad to bring you. Wait here a second."

Magnolia sipped the water and waited for the woman to return. She stared at the framed college degrees on the wall, two of them, with the name Rebecca Delmonico written in fancy lettering. Photos surrounded the degrees—the woman next to dogs, horses, parrots, an iguana, and even a tiger. The smell of baking grew stronger and she heard the woman talking a couple of rooms away, then the oven timer beeping. The woman pulled something out of an oven, and she finally returned.

"Let's get you in the truck."

"He said okay?"

"He said he couldn't hear me and hung up, so we'll go ask him ourselves. I know where it is."

Magnolia began to limp but Rebecca lifted her with surprising ease, smiling at the young girl's reaction.

"I've birthed calves bigger than you and hauled a Great Dane up a fifty-foot ravine after a car wreck once. They look big and tough but they're just babies when they get scared."

Rebecca helped her ease into the passenger seat of an old Chevy pickup truck with soft, cracked leather seats, warm but not scalding. Rebecca shoved a pile of work gloves and papers out of the way and got behind the wheel, pulling out onto a quiet, twisting back road. The sky was turning light purple to the east and long striations of gray clouds blotted out the setting sun, making the road a little darker than it should have been before dusk.

"So what brought you out this way?" the doctor asked. "It's pretty rugged out there behind my place."

"I was looking for something."

Rebecca waited. "Something you lost?"

Magnolia felt her face go red. "No, a house. I was looking for a house in the Dominion."

Rebecca glanced at her, her eyes looking for more but careful not to make the girl any more embarrassed.

"Well, it's pretty easy to get turned around back in there. You know if you head north of here it just goes for miles until you hit Camp Bullis? They do military training out there. Huge stretches of nothing for survivalist exercises, so I'm glad you ended up in my backyard."

"Me too," Magnolia whispered to herself.

She closed her eyes and ran her hands over the seat. It felt much more comfortable than the one in her father's truck, which he'd repaired numerous times with frayed duct tape. Soon Rebecca turned into an area Magnolia recognized as the far end of her neighborhood, and it surprised her how far she had walked through the heat and hills in her frightened delirium. As they approached the corner where the Silver Fox sat back from the road, the streetlights overhead all came on at once, a magical little moment she only saw now and again, and it always made Magnolia smile. They slowed, rolling into the uneven dirt lot. The lights illuminated the old trucks and jeeps while also casting shadows deeper beneath the trees. Rebecca parked her truck along the road away from the others and told Magnolia to wait.

Magnolia watched her walk away, her gait steady and assured, not at all like her father's slumped wavering on his way out to his own truck each day. Rebecca disappeared through the trucks and into the cinder-block tavern's door as golden light streamed into the dirt lot. She could hear the faint jauntiness of country music, maybe Dwight Yoakam. She couldn't be sure. A minute later Rebecca came out and walked around the back of the building. Then nothing.

Magnolia grew anxious, shifting in the warm seat, and finally she decided to follow her, slipping out the Chevy door and limping gently through the row of trucks and around the side of the tavern, past the propane tanks and garbage cans until she saw Rebecca standing over a man lying on the bench seat of a picnic table. The man lazily waved a hand and slurred something she couldn't understand, but when she recognized the boots and flannel shirt, she knew it was her father. Rebecca helped him sit up, but he pushed her away. She replied with something terse and turned, spotting Magnolia and waving at her to follow her back to the parking lot.

"He's too drunk to understand what I'm even saying."

"Should we help him?"

They paused and looked back. Her father was rubbing his head and leaning back against the table. Rebecca said, "No," and took Magnolia's hand, then she stopped and moved to pick her up again.

"C'mon, you shouldn't be on your feet."

"I can walk."

Rebecca considered it. "Just be careful. Go slow."

"I'll ask him to take me to the doctor tomorrow. He's always better in the morning."

"You shouldn't wait."

"He might be mad if I go without him."

"How mad will he be when he wakes up and he has to drive you into San Antonio?"

166

Magnolia considered that. "Pretty mad either way."

They stopped and stood by the truck, the engine ticking in the heat, the country music drifting through the night air and crickets. Magnolia recognized Garth Brooks singing about all his friends in low places.

"You live nearby?" Rebecca asked.

"Yes."

"Show me."

It was a short drive, less than a minute, and Magnolia watched the guard house by the Dominion gate for signs of life as Rebecca pulled into the cul-de-sac. The trailer homes around hers were lit up by glowing television lights switching blue and white, but her own stood dark and silent.

"That one," she told Rebecca, who walked right up to the door and went inside.

Something about that surprised and embarrassed Magnolia, as if the woman hadn't just barged into her father's trailer but her own private sanctum. She limped after and found Rebecca looking around the living room, hands on her hips. Magnolia's face went red again when she too saw the room through the veterinarian's eyes: spoiling food on the table, cigarettes stubbed out on the floor, the smell of garbage, roaches skittering into the darker corners, black mold speckling the wall near the bathroom door.

"You're coming with me," Rebecca said.

"Where?"

"Just c'mon."

Magnolia felt that wave of embarrassment again, shame and guilt, and she rushed into her bedroom, slamming the door behind her. The door sounded cheap and hollow now, and the room looked as bad as the rest of the house, a nest of filth and clothes, bedsheets unwashed for months, broken furniture, old

167

Sunkist pouches scattered about. Rebecca knocked, calling for her, not quite pleading or demanding, but calm and direct.

"I'm not saying I'm taking you away for good, but I'm taking you someplace clean so we can take care of that foot. You need to get a shot or infection is going to set in."

"My dad will take me," Magnolia said, but she could hear the uncertainty in her voice.

"Look around at how he takes care of his house. If he takes care of your foot like this, you'll lose your foot. You might even lose your leg. You could even die if you wait long enough. Do you want to lie on the floor here dying hoping he comes home sober enough to bring you to the ER? I know that's mean to say, but I'm being honest with you."

Magnolia held the door shut with her shoulder and stared through her bedroom window, out into the darkened side yard cut through with a pink-orange wave of streetlight. Grime and nose prints streaked the window. She couldn't see anything out there but light and dark shapes. Her whole life just light and dark shapes, nothing distinct, nothing certain. She thought of her father out there in the nigh, sitting in his own hazy drunkenness, and of her mother somewhere further, somewhere deep underground. She closed her eyes and heard Rebecca asking her again if she trusted her father to do the right thing.

Magnolia opened the door.

"I'm not judging you," Rebecca said. "I just don't want you to get sick. I can't just go home and let that happen."

"He doesn't look at me when he talks to me," Magnolia said. "He hasn't looked at me since mom died."

Rebecca squatted, her eyes warm and brown in the streetlight coming through the front door. She asked, "How long ago was that?"

"Almost two years."

Rebecca nodded and held out her hand. They walked to the truck together, climbed inside, and left the cul-de-sac behind. Magnolia closed her eyes as they passed the Silver Fox again and didn't open them until they were on the highway heading south. It was almost full night, and to their left beyond the highway and the long iron fence she saw lights in the hills, the distant mansions of the Dominion. She told Rebecca about the man who owned his own private water park, a lazy river, and the snack bar that served nachos. That's why she was in the wilderness. She just wanted to see it. Just a quick look to know if something like that was real.

Rebecca glanced toward the hills too, then turned back to the empty highway leading toward San Antonio. The distant lights of downtown grew into a great dome of orange in the purple-black sky. For a few minutes neither said a word, and Magnolia noticed how much older and tired Rebecca looked in the light of the dashboard. It made her like Rebecca more, somehow, the hardening of one's armor against the coming night. The toughness. The truth.

"Magnolia, that man is a multi-millionaire who puts a ball in a hoop for a living. And your father, I don't know what he does, but I see how he lives, and it might sound crazy to you, but I don't have much more respect for one over the other. It's just men playing games while they run out the clock. And where are you in all this?"

"I don't know," Magnolia said, uncertain of what the veterinarian was getting at.

"Wandering in the hills alone, looking for the end of the fence, looking for a magical house with a water park, and falling down into a ditch with the rest of the garbage men throw away. Here, hold this."

Rebecca took Magnolia's hand and set it on the wheel, then let her own hands go. Magnolia almost panicked at the realization she was driving the truck one-handed going almost seventy-five miles per hour, but the truck stayed steady, stayed in the middle lane of the three-lane highway. Her heart beat wild and her foot throbbed again. The lights of San Antonio grew larger in the sky.

"Who's in control of your life right now?"

Magnolia swallowed hard. "I am."

"When is the last time you felt that way?"

"Never."

"Not once?"

"No, never."

Rebecca gently placed her hands on the wheel again, but Magnolia didn't remove hers for another full minute, then settled back into the seat, staring dead ahead at those lights, blue exit signs flying past them.

"You're going to find a lot of fences in your life, a lot of gates, a lot of ditches full of garbage, a lot of boys more worried about nachos and getting drunk, and not one of them is going to steer your life any better than you can. You might meet one or two who might help, but you're the only one at the wheel, understand?"

Magnolia nodded.

"When we get to urgent care, let me talk to them. I know the doctors there and they'll fix you up. Then we're going to go have something to eat and have a long talk about what comes next."

"What comes next?"

Rebecca accelerated the truck and glanced at Magnolia, taking her hands off the wheel and holding them up, waiting. Magnolia reached over and placed her left hand on the wheel, her heartbeat pounding again, her eyes never leaving the highway leading south into the bright lights and concrete tangle of the city, her life moving forward with relentless speed and will.

The Majestic

in the scintillation of the marquee lights
the crowds leave the sidewalk heat behind,
summer colors and desert nights behind,
chaos and bombs falling behind,
    to enter The Majestic

a ghost and a memory carry tickets
arm in arm toward the lobby lights,
blinded by then neon illumination red
and white striations upon the milling infinitesimal
universes gravitating around love and debt and hunger
and petty little nothingness, whispered
en masse while congregating in waves
    to enter The Majestic

as we, the ghost and the memory,
ascend toward the astrological decadence,
past marble pillars and brass stanchions,
towards angled seats beneath walls of blue velvet
and ceilings of sunsets, stars, palatial vistas
dimming as curtains rise, casting us
into a real where time and our inevitable ends
could not touch us, could not find us,
lost beneath the balconies and gilded stars

theatre, the ecclesiastical wonderment of the arts
gives such blessings if you hold dear to
catechisms pure, to marvels true, to fables raw,
if you give yourself to the leaps of fantasy
plumbing the human depths of war,
depravity, love, and all the reasons
    for our mortal pageantry

but when we rise for the final applause

we realize, each quietly to ourselves,
that all things must occur along all timelines,
certainties in abundance

though I hold out hope that somewhere
along one of those infinite strands of existence
the play goes on in a life unwritten,
act after act in the embrace of the dark
while outside the marquee lights
    of The Majestic shine
in unrequited splendor
for just a little longer,
just a little longer

Texas Songbirds

I feel them, this series of
heartbeats conjoined
into endless stoplights
fighting the blue dawn memory
of waking hard-pressed for air and
holding on to the mattress until it stops
spinning into the wild, palms hard
against sterile white walls

the birds outside understand,
they wait
silent among the white crape myrtles,
knowing all flowering trees will bloom each
year until they are cut down and die

but the soft morning light tells me I live,
the pain in my heart tells me I live,
the flashing blue light on my phone
tells me I live and will live another night
as soon as I rise to make ready

the ghosts of Saturday night may carry me
into the next stoplight mad-rush neon head-long
into brambles of bourbon and lipstick

but it is the hope of quiet mornings with you
somewhere far from those Texas songbirds
that makes me push myself from the soft
blue sheets of today and aim my
conjoined heartbeats toward a tomorrow
where new blue dawn memories await

Death & Co.

of course, it's only a matter of time

so much of the city is already crowded
by ghosts and shadows that move
from one room to the next, even
my father's house is occupied by
spirits who don't want us in her home

it's like that everywhere: in the
hotel downtown, the one famous for
those murders, the man who carried
body parts out of his room in suitcases

or the bar on the west side that is no
longer in operation, where shadow
you and shadow me sit and collect
dust as we wait for the bartender
to refill our glasses with bourbon

or the walls of the Alamo downtown
crawling with the screams of those
men who died in hellfire and dirt,
some say for freedom, others say
to skip taxes or rip the land away from
those who had lived there first, but there's
always someone who came first, and
their ghosts are there too, watching the hellfire
consume us all in the south Texas heat

I know there will come a day
when there won't be any reason
for me to return, some final funeral,
and I'll bring my last bag out
to the sidewalk and wait for a car as

ghosts drift by in the cobalt blue skies

but maybe the pain of knowing
an empty city is waiting for me
down south won't overcome my
curiosity to return, walk those rooms,
those bars, those landmarks to listen
to the whispers of Death & Co. one
more time before I too cross the river
at night to join them, in just a matter
of time

Stonehedge

their home stood near the end of the block,
a low flat house of white, a garage, a car port,
and if you listen you might hear wind chimes,
cicadas calling from the twisted oak branches,
a screen door in the back yard, you might
smell water warmed by a green rubber hose
and flowers in dozens of pots large and small
filling a shaded patio where at night the
moonflowers and evening primrose open
to the soft dew of the stars, and children
whisper to their grandmothers for another
can of soda, another hour beside her in
the glow of the television light, and then
all falls quiet on Stonehedge Drive as the
centuries pass and the slumber of ageless
gods continue uninterrupted by love or
death or the idle years that wait between
filled with soft miracles and summer nights

Lackland

Kit-Kat candy bar in the morning mist;
he walks me 'round the decommissioned
war planes, transports, spotters, wheels
held by chains and concrete, noses pointing
toward the skies as we move from one
to the next and I watch him, his soft beard
and gentle hands that hold mine, then I spot
a jackrabbit across the field, watching us

he says I can go chase it but I only walk
toward the jackrabbit until it speeds away
and dives into a theretofore unseen hole
and I turn to my grandfather who is now
walking to the next plane, the mist clearing
as the Texas sun warms the air and earth
and my skin, and between the planes, my grandad,
the jackrabbits, and the fading morning mist, I
wonder what of all this will remain and what will
fade as if it never existed—and just like that:
I run

The Daredevil

Sometimes if you stayed at Sea World until the very
end of the night when most families are heading to
their cars and many of the small concession stands and
gift shops are closing up, the ride operators will come
onto the PA system and say, "You want to go around
one last time?"

Yes, of course we do, my sister and I fortunate
enough to score season passes for the first and last time
in our lives at ages nine and twelve. Sometimes the
operators asked this when we were soaking wet on the
Raging River, swirling in the giant round tubes, water
sloshing in the bottom and bloating our sneakers and
socks. Granny might ride that one with us now and
then, but usually she would stand on the bridge
overlooking the river and watch for us. Even in the
darkness of that last half hour of the park, we'd see her
and she'd see us and we'd all wave as music played
through speakers disguised as boulders and the rushing
torrents would spin us away out of her sight and into
the oncoming waterfalls that would make us scream
with delight.

The other ride was something a little more mythic,
a little more dangerous. The Log Flume. At night the
rattling machinery that would carry our logs up into the
air felt almost malignant, aware, hungry. The
shuddering of the log escalator only made our
anticipation more intense. Granny never rode this one,
but Grandad would. He would sit in the back and one
or two of us would sit in the front, holding on to the
edge with fingers damp, claw-like, and desperate. High
in the night skies of south Texas, the orange dome of
San Antonio visible once we rose above the treeline,
and then the small splash into the roiling waters of the

179

half-tube carrying us through the skies, the log bumping the sides, water splashing up into our seats.

Grandad was a daredevil, especially in his old age. He would jump up in elevators as they rose, making them groan and creak, terrifying everyone on board. He would rock gondolas back and forth as they cradled us over rivers and gardens, the cable moaning as he laughed, calling out his delighted, "Whoaaaaaahhhh!" And as the log flume turned through its runs and curves, he'd rock with it, letting the water splash higher, causing us to tilt and *klonk* into the sides with greater velocity. Then he smiled with glee as we neared the big drop.

"Here we goooo!" he'd declare, and down we went, rushing through the water at 45 degrees, or what felt like a straight drop, his hands in the air as we screamed.

But he didn't always do that. Sometimes, just the two of us, my grandad in the back, me in the front, and he'd sit quietly and stare off toward the city's glowing horizon, while in all other directions the Texas wilderness stood in blackened contrast. The breeze at night at those heights, the gentle sloshing of the water, the causal bump of our log as it floated through the flume, and my Grandad looking off into the lights. If they'd let us, I'd ride that portion over and over and over until dawn, to be with him there in that silence.

But no matter how many times we basked in those somnolent moments up in the Texas skies, the big drop always came, and he'd always say, "Here we goooo!"

And down we went, into the waters below, into the walkways and parking lots, into the highways and into bed, into tomorrow and into the next school year, into college and into life and into funeral parlors and into the grave.

When he died in 2001, I lived in Albany. I was a poor college student and he was back in Texas. My family said not to worry, it was sudden and it was over. I stayed home, but I always wished I had gone to see him. Maybe it was best that I didn't. I never had to look down into his coffin and say, "It doesn't even look like him." I never had to deal with my cousin, who also got drunk and obnoxious at my Granny's funeral a decade later. I never had to cry as strangers shook my hand and said they were sorry.

Instead, I open my eyes and I see the Texas stars at night, feel the log slipping through the flume, bumping along in the dark as the wind and water rushes us ever forward. And I know he's behind me, holding the sides of our log, looking off into the horizon, or maybe even looking at me.

And when the big drop comes, I know what he'll say. And even if I close my eyes on the way down, I'll be ready.

Together in the Fire

give me an evening, take me
  down past the hotels
    and mansions and gnarled
      exits ramps, walk me through
the crowds at the cantinas,
  the rows of parked motorcycles,
    the lights strung orange and golden,
      beer in green bottles, brown,
lead me over gravel lots past
  railroad tracks in the dark all
    the way to Blue Star crowds in
      cement-walled warehouses, the
galleries splayed with paintings, murals,
  birds and skeletal wires in the shapes
    of heartbeats and burning avenues,
      and all of them look like love,
it's love, all of these friendships, all of these
  nights with you, with us, with the mesmerized
    crowds of people moving through the
      night into random parties, conversations
with local art heroes about their experiences
  with aliens, with abductions not of body
    but of spirit, and all the walls somehow
      turn into art right before our eyes
give me those nights, prowling through blue
  neon poolhalls and beerhalls and have
    you met Javier? have you met Gabriella?
    have you been to the Jazz Annex after midnight?
those nights, kicked out of one bar and greeted
  by name at the next, drinks ready before we even
    hit the stool, and on the television we see scenes
      from Fiesta, something between Mardi Gras
and a county fair, packed streets, dancing, drunks,
  paper lanterns and El Ray blessing our hangovers,

then it's the Spurs: is it 2007? is it 2014? are we on
our way? give me lost voices screaming in joy
give me the night, the glow from one horizon to the
next, the highways reeling, driving from our small
trailer in Boerne to Gran's house on the southside,
give me her smile as I walk in, say hello, embrace,
watch the Oscars on a night so cool we can open
all the windows and the doors for once, don't mind
the moths, let them see the glamour, let them hear
my granny flirt with Hugh Jackman once more,
give that to me, the night drives in Alamo Heights
through Castle Hills, Leon Valley and Monte Vista,
give me alleyway print shops with impromptu
salons painters, poets, braggarts, and love, love,
everyone wearing "Keep San Antonio Lame"
t-shirts, and me too, I'm there, it happened
and the warmth of it all, not just the endless nights
of scintillation rising from the pavement, not just
the burn of the tequila after our eighth shot that hour,
but the comraderies innumerable, immeasurable, in
any direction and any hour, even when alone in
the car with nowhere to go but drive the 410 Loop
as Jack Kerouac reads poetry between Miles Davis
improvisations, we're together in the fire pulsing,
give me those nights and more, let me be greedy
let me love this city with all my heart,
just one more time

May the Moon Shine On

may the moon shine on
may the oak trees rattle
may the cats sleep in the
shadows of the rose bush

may the lights of the drive-thru
taco joints along Nacogdoches
shine on beneath that gold moon

may the din of highway traffic
hold the walls of this citadel up
for another year, another century,
long enough for our sad redemption

may the crickets in the soft yellow
glow of my father's porch light on
Sagebrush Lane orchestrate their
celestial infinities for as many heat
waves and floods as they can survive

may you and I end with good-bye
and not some painful silence that
will haunt us into every karmic life
that may follow this heartbreak of
human existence we call our city

may the moon shine on
may the rains come gentle
may the mission bells toll
whatever warning they can
when our last night comes

may the wind carry their sound
may the cats wake in time to hear it

may the moon shine on
may the moon shine on

Loop 410

one long pure circle of death and memory
who am I to tell you even one story?

listen to the miracle of endless drives home, the
traffic after dusk, neon signs like gravestones for sale

nobody told the weeds to crawl through
the cracks of the offramp, nobody says much at all

we're born, we die, we circle the loop
in search of black bean tacos and solace

halogen fire switchblade every street and exit
with deep gashes of midnight and darkness

you can hear it when you don't move
you can hear it when it moves through you

you can feel it sideswipe your 3 p.m.
and send you to church to pray for your soul

you can't get lost and you can't get born
you can only change at I-10, I-35, 281

around and around and around you can keep
going around but it's only your journey

the rest of the highways exist to careen
and sway and ascend around Loop 410

see the boots by the mall, almost thirty feet tall?
see the castle and go-carts and 12-year-old you

standing beneath the stars, this child asks, *is it*

impossible to be this happy forever?

eat your tacos and don't ask for a thing
and maybe the centuries will be kind

only one way to find out
full tank, ten million stars

deep in the heart of TX,
we'll get lost

where the mind won't find us,
at last

Barmacy

it stood on the corner of Hildebrandt
and McCollough, that part of town they built
in the 1930s, *streamline moderne* as they say,
everything looking five decades past its peak
yet retaining some sort of worn dignity,
some style, some aerodynamic charm

by day it was a working pharmacy, little rows
of shelves with toiletries, pills, bandages,
cleaning products and pantyhose, and
it even had a little lunch counter with maybe
a dozen stools, the spinning kind
with no backs, and you could have coffee
and eggs or a BLT and read a newspaper, back
when people would just read newspapers

but by night they turned an open area
in the rear into a makeshift stage, and
they'd have poets read, or folk singers,
or comedians telling bad jokes, or
sometimes even small garage bands
and people could hang out, buy a beer
from out of a cooler and see a little show
or read a little poetry, but it was never
all too crowded, being in an odd place

it was pretty far from the college bars
on St. Mary's or the dives up on Blanco
and far too far from downtown, just
tucked away amongst the palm trees and
old car lots and strings of *streamline
moderne* shopfronts that later became
law firms, tax preparers, bail bondsmen,
and the like, places that close early and

stay closed on the weekends, and so

over the years we went less and less and
not long after I left town I heard the old
barmacy had closed permanently, but
nothing took its place, it just sits there,
the curved neon signage wrapping around
the front façade, the sunbeaten stucco
cracking and falling into the weed-filled
parking lot as San Antonio churns ever
onward into the future, the poets and
the coffee drinkers and the punks all
finding other places to read and rage
until the hungry years come for them too

It's Too Late to Turn Back

here we go, highway bound again
through months and years that
eat their own tails, circling back around
to fresh hells burning old landscapes
in Texas and California and New
York City and the heat radiating from
sidewalk nightclub poolroom madness where
I last saw you and felt the
world pulsing through filaments overhead
streetlight heartbeats and heartbreaks
gone now to the hungry years
friends gone to graves
love gone to folly
peace gone to riots
all our dreams gone to highway miles,
off to find some sort of escape, the
mile marker canyon yawning
mountain looming prairie slumbering
away the ecstasies of life,
lamented ecstasies every mile,
a little closer to the end now,
the radio playing that same old
Replacements song somewhere
far to the left of the dial, fighting
the static, holding off the last exit for
just a little longer, the highway
thinning out, the dial turning
deeper yet into that fiery sunset
where the sky meets the sea,
and where maybe
you and I will meet again
if the road gods of karma
deem it so

Little Victory Diner

Wanda wiped the counter with a blue cloth and watched the kid walk through the diner door. Maybe not a kid, but definitely not a man. With floppy black hair and thick glasses, and teeth too straight to not have had braces on them within the last couple of years. He looked like a nebulous being who could chameleon his way between fourteen or twenty-five, she figured, depending on what clothes he wore or how straight he sat up. But the way he dragged himself to the counter with such a loose, rubbery exhaustion, she pegged him for a runaway who'd reached the end of line.

"Coffee?" she asked, expecting him to order a pop instead, but he nodded. She slid him a menu. "You look wore out, young man."

"I am. You still open for a while?"

She said yes, but understood why he asked. The only other occupants of the diner were JT and Mary Wentworth, who arrived every night after nine o'clock for pie and ice cream and always sat in the back booth. The busboy had called out three minutes before his shift was supposed to start and the cook went home the hour prior with a stomach bug, so Wanda was alone. But since it was just another quiet weeknight in little ol' Alpine, she figured she could hold the fort on her own.

She'd been right. It had been dead all night and she was happy to have the kid to serve. There were only so many times you could wipe down the same counter.

"So what's it gonna be?" she asked

"Got any pie left?"

"I got a slice of pecan, and a couple slices of blueberry left. We close in an hour so the choices are pretty slim."

"Blueberry," he said, sipping his coffee.

She watched his face when he did, to see if he actually drank coffee or just sipped it to look the part, but he didn't skip a beat.

"Quiet night, huh?"

"You're a regular Columbo," she said.

"A what?"

"Detective."

"Oh, right. I mean, I saw the hotels were all packed so I thought the diner would be too."

"You'd think," Wanda said, sliding him a plate of pie. "But most folks who pass through going to Big Bend or the observatory or whatnot just hit the McDonald's or Pizza Hut. We'd like the business but since it's just me tonight I guess I don't mind the break."

The kid nodded while he ate his pie. Ate was an understatement. The way he wolfed down forkful after forkful made her double-down on the runaway story. JT and Mary stood up from their green vinyl booth and he helped her with her jacket before they waved goodnight. Wanda waved back and glanced past them outside at the hotels across and up the street, every one full up. Some of the windows had blinds partially shut, leaving a crack. Others showed TV lights glowing, jumping from blue to white to darkness, then back to blue. But there wasn't a soul on the sidewalks.

"Gets this way after eight or so," Wanda said to no one in particular while she emptied one of the two coffee machines, dumping the filters and grounds into a can. "Dinner crowd is gone, travelers are tired, locals are in bed."

"Why do you stay open?"

"Folks like you. There's always one or two." She looked at the last slice of blueberry pie and shoveled it onto a new plate, then slid it over to him. "You look like a good eater. That one's on the house."

"Really? Thanks," he said, immediately starting in on it.

"Well ain't you hungrier than a starved dog. Where are you from?"

"New York City."

"What? How the hell did ya end up in the backside'a Texas?"

"Long story."

"It's a long hour left till we're closed. What's your name anyway?"

"Jim."

"Wanda."

"I can tell. The name tag."

She glanced down. "Wanda so far as you know. This could just be a ruse."

"Is it?"

"I'll let you keep guessin'. So how'd you get so far from home?"

"I hate it there," he said, working in another bite of pie. "The noise never stops. The lights blot out the sky. The winters freeze your soul right out of your body. And the summers are just as bad, everything just stinks like garbage and everyone's mad about it. The honking, the shouting. I just couldn't take it anymore. I asked a librarian what the quietest, darkest spot in America was and she said to take your pick, northern Montana or Big Bend out in Texas. I was tired of being cold, so I picked Texas."

"It'll get hot again here soon enough."

"Yeah, but a clean kind of hot, I can tell."

"Maybe, but what do you expect to do here now that you made it?"

His eyes lowered and he chewed the last bite. He didn't answer.

"Big secret, huh? Hold up the bank and live off the fat of the land, I expect. Maybe I should call the sheriff."

She thought she'd get a smile out of him, but he just stared at his plate.

"Want more coffee?"

"No thanks."

"Want more food?"

"I—I should be honest, I guess. Before I go much further with it. I—I don't have any money."

"I see."

"I had some, but this guy, he took it."

"Who did?'

"Some guy in a white pickup. He gave me a lift in Fort Stockton and about halfway here he stopped, shook me down for my money, and kicked me out. I spent the whole day walking the rest of the way here. I'm real sorry."

Wanda hesitated, scanning his face for a lie, but he seemed sincere. Still...

"Well, damn, maybe I really *should* call the sheriff."

She expected him to protest, his bluff called, but he just looked up and shrugged.

"I thought about it," he said. "but it was only fifty bucks. The guy had New Mexico plates too, so I wasn't sure he was local. I don't know, you think they'd believe me?"

"Maybe, but I don't think anyone's puttin' up roadblocks for no fifty bucks."

"I'd be happy to work this pie off."

"Just you sit there and rest. Sounds like a long walk. You like pecan pie?"

"Yeah but I don't want anymore. I can't pay."

"I wasn't chargin' you anyway," she said, digging the slice out of the aluminum dish onto a plate. "No, c'mon now, just sit."

But he was already up, clearing the dishes on the booth where the Wentworth couple had been, wiping a few drips of ice cream with a napkin. He walked the bowls and silverware over and she directed him toward the sink, telling him to just drop them in, but he got to washing them and then started in on the others she'd piled up over the night. She scolded him and insisted he stop but he just said, "I'll stop when I've paid off three slices and a coffee."

Wanda gave up and watched him work for a minute, scrubbing away at plates and pot and spoons. She turned to the coffee machines and figured he was safe enough working on his own, and even if he wasn't, there wasn't but nearly fifteen dollars in the register anyway. Big deal.

"If you were looking for quiet, you came to the right place," she said, tying up garbage bags and setting them by the back door. "You can hear the bats fly at midnight and the sun creak through at noon. I sure wish I could hear a little of that New York racket every now and then."

"You're better off," Jim said, drying his hands. "I took all I could and all I wanted was to get—ah, never mind."

"What?"

He hesitated. "You guys have a movie theater in town?"

"You came all this way for a movie?"

"No, I—it's a nice place. I was walking around, looking at things. You even got a little college, I saw."

"Yeah, that's true. It's tiny but it's here. And a one-screen theater. And a bowling alley if you're ambitious. What's the matter anyway?"

Jim was staring out the windows across the diner at the hotels all lit up, the trucks and cars lining the wide downtown street. He looked even more tired than when he walked in.

"I came out to the desert to walk out into it, to feel it, experience it, sit and listen to nothing, and just keep going until I vanished. I was done with all the people and noise, the lights and fighting, the hate and politics."

"There ain't no gettin' away from politics," she said. "You'll get out there and the stumps will start stump speechin' at ya, askin' for money too."

"I was going to kill myself out there."

She stared at the back of his head for a long minute, then sighed.

"Well...shit, don't go doin' something foolish like that. You're just a boy. You don't know what kinda mischief you got left."

"I was going to do it, but the further away from New York I got, I guess I started wavering. And walking through town here, I never felt like I do now. It's different. It's like I can turn around and disappear but not really be gone. It's like I can breathe again."

"That's a good hobby to hold on to."

"You always work alone?"

"No. We lost a busboy tonight. And I can tell by the way you washed those plates, you're overqualified, so I don't even want to hear you complain when I tell you about the ungodly high wages and unparalleled cuisines you'll be party to when you come on back tomorrow."

He laughed in a tame self-aware sort of way, and Wanda felt a sense of relief to finally see him smile.

"I don't even know what I'm doing out here now," he said, leaning against the counter. "I had this whole plan and now I don't know."

"Well you grab that broom and I'll grab this mop and we'll see if we can't figure out the world's problems between us while we close up. And then we'll figure out yours too. How's that sound?"

"I'll work off that pie, not a problem."

"I expect you already have. C'mon, this floor ain't going to sparkle by itself."

He took the broom and walked to the far corner of the diner, and she watched him sweep while her bucket filled with hot water. Outside, the hotel lights began to turn off behind orange curtains one after another, and inside the scent of pine floor cleaner filled the air in a way that always made her think of her grandmother, bless her soul, and the way she'd always snap at her granddaddy to take his boots off at the door after a long day of hauling junk. Little victories that she hoped added up to something worthwhile, someday.

Later, when she locked the glass door of the darkened diner and stood in the still-warm parking lot, she looked up at the stars and the young man beside her did the same.

"I expect you don't have any place to sleep tonight?"

"Not really, but I've been sleeping rough and I don't mind it."

"You'll mind *me* if I catch you doing that around here. C'mon. My brother lives ten doors down behind his repair shop. Junking and fixin' cars runs in my family, all the way back to Henry Ford, I expect. He'll put you up, has one of those 'man caves' with an extra couch. He's a talker though, and he'll be happy to have a new ear to chew on."

"I appreciate it."

"I expect so," Wanda said. "But don't you thank me 'til after he gnaws on you about the glory days of the Cowboys for the umpteenth time."

Their shadows waxed and waned, casting about as they passed lit-up porches and darkened parking lots, distant streetlights and the yonder moon above. And for a short stretch there wasn't anything across the street but the rumpled, rugged ground running off toward a distant plateau, silhouetted by stars and the pearlescent Milky Way pouring through the sky like one long miracle leading into forever. She smelled sage and dirt, heard a distant train and then nothing but their feet, and Wanda supposed she could understand why someone would want to go get lost in all that. In a way she knew she'd go find the limits of all that darkness and stars too one day, but just making it to the end of each day at this point in life was a little victory all its own.

Glancing at the boy as they neared her brother's shop with its cottage behind, she hoped very much that Jim would show up in the diner the next day. For food or a job or just to talk. If he did, another victory. And if not...well, the universe held answers for everyone, and sometimes those answers came in looking for pie, and sometimes they were out there hiding in the hills. Only one way to find out which.

She gave Jim a wink, knocked on the door, and waited.

whatever the night might bring

the hours sink into aftermath,
badger and pull the seconds
down and away and gone and
I depend on dreams to unknot
the threads of incongruent ills
and thermonuclear desires but
in truth the only way beyond
the bramble & chaos is straight
through, headlong into dark, the
abyss, the loss of control, giving
ourselves over to whatever the
night might bring in the relentless
Texan heat, lying helpless on
linen bedsheets and regret as
hours sink into aftermath, as
dawn hunts for us across the miles
like the last savior we'll never know,
forever out of reach until we rise at
last & burn upon re-entry, our ash
forgotten; our radiation so pure

Maps & Legends

orange halogen dust bowl
across the southern horizon
as San Antonio hums with
highways and even in the dark
pockets of the city behind
fences and culverts, the crickets
and cicadas orchestrate a hounding call,
so soft and rhythmic
against the lapping waves
of heat that holds the city hostage
through every calendar month,
every hour, every lifetime

westward the sun gives way
to purple night and the hills
rolls and hide forgotten dreams
in every arroyo and ravine,
small ranch homes twinkling
in the night, grayed abuelas
limping to bed after too many
years of children and lotto tickets,
hail storms and small town skies
where the milky way opens
up its arms and sends a wave
of majesty down to the dusty
prickly lawns and little patios
full of cacti in red clay pots

if you can see beyond
the flatland miles to the east, past the
Houston megachurches and exit ramps
and skyscrapers, there's a jungle
of swampland and forests, old boxcars idling
on abandoned spurs, the wood

creaking in the wind as another
stormfront moves through the valleys
and cotton fields, through
the demons and the sins of humanity,
through the white-spired
churches dotting the small towns
named after Greek cities, the
promises of each almost forgotten
in the aching maw of life

and if I stand in that darkened
back yard on the north edge of
San Antonio in early spring I can
sometimes smell the pine
trees of home, the dead needles
waiting for spring rains to call
to the seedling grass, the soft
cool sunlight beckoning them to
ascend through the soil, the budding
affirmations that seasons
still change somewhere,
that endings have beginnings,
that nothing stays down for too long,
no matter how lost one
might become, maps cast away
and the stars above keeping
their secrets until the very end,
when we each find home at last

Riverwalk

winter jazz nights alongside black waters dancing red
blue green white in all possible Christmas variations,
fiesta phosphorescent, the smell of late night fajitas and
red wine ebbing in the wind that slips through stone
bridges crossing the narrow river snaking through the
heart of downtown, a palm tree canopy overhead, little
hollows and coves tucked below street-level traffic,
grotto solitude where shadows and a lonely cello
somewhere soften his touch along your hairline, running
one long black curl behind your ear, smiling as I pass by
and turn my eyes away into the night, allowing as much
intimacy as one can along the Riverwalk, escaping into
the darkness of another bridge and stone steps leading
me up into halogen yellow streets engulfed by a sudden
warm wind, rare for December, though this is south
Texas, where heat and a soft caress in the night are so
mundane the stars deign not one glimpse down through
the cloudless sky, only burn burn burn lifetimes away as
their own hearts die a slow fiery death, cautionary tales
a million times over, should we care to notice, but we
don't, we won't, and the river trembles onward through
fiesta neon midnight

Southern Tectonic

atmospheric consumption
heat ruminant with immensity
casting far and wide across
prairie and hill and ravine and
sky, an embrace giving you
everything you never felt in the arms
of those you loved and lost
and left behind in cities east and west
and even right here, deep
in the sweltering heart of Texas

stand and take it, feel it, hold it
101 degrees even at midnight as you
close your eyes in the middle
of the road in your aging father's
neighborhood on the north end
of town, hold it, feel it, take
it, this heat is for you, smelting your
bones to iron ore, baking
your soul into something harder
something that will last you all the
remaining miles of your life

take all that burning immensity
the shifting plates within your heart
hold it tight with both your arms

and run

And the Party Never Ends

if you leave San Antonio around 4 a.m.
you might make that Mad-Max run up to
Austin with almost no traffic, maybe a semi
or two, but that's it, and I eased from one
lane to the next in a state of anxious luxury,
looking forward to and worried about another
trek up through Waco, Dallas, Little Rock,
Memphis, Nashville, the Smokies, then the
choice of Virginia flatlands or West Virginia
switchbacks, and it doesn't matter which
because by then you're a zombie to the road,
the fever dreams, the white pills that keep you
running headlong, the picnic tables at rest stops
that become your funeral slabs for 30 minute naps
in the open air, then back to the highway dreams

but that morning, close to 4:30 a.m. just
outside of San Antonio, I had the road alone,
the radio tuned to some no-name station
that started to play Robert Earl Keen,
"The Road That Never Ends," and as it
flowed through speakers in the far edge of
night I felt the wheels of the car begin to lift
right off the blacktop, the tale of Sonny and
and Sherry, Main Street after midnight, a beer
between her legs as she's off to meet some
friends, how the party never ends…

as the horizon became a cobalt blue zipper
ready to peel open another bright sky highway
that song carried me past the anxieties that had
built and strangled and followed me all the way
from my father's front steps, carried me beyond
my fears of making another mistake, leaving one

home behind to re-start my life back at my other,
both ways home feeling more like emergency
parachutes than anything, but ol' Robert Earl Keene
kept singing and I kept driving, and you know what?

he's right, the road goes on forever, even when you
wish it wouldn't, even after you take that last exit,
be it another big mistake or the best decision you
ever made, when you're nothing but highway dust,
that party will still be out there beyond the horizon
at 5:05 a.m., threatening another bright blue day
without your bones walking around to greet it

there's a little comfort in that, I think,
but only if you turn the radio up and
keep moving forward with all the speed
and hope and wild grace you can muster

Turn the Lantern Low

I have a desert hilltop dream
where structure and silence align
        the days and nights
crawl like stone
across the grassland
        cut by canyons and arroyo,
empty western highways,
pine and stone and sky

at night the moon illuminates nothing
save the expanse of everything we don't know,
the stars like grains of white hot sand
tossed into the midnight sea

I saw this place once as a child
I dreamt of this place ever since,
of a house on that desert hilltop

I go there
at night and sit
and listen to the ghosts ride
the ever-present wind,
dead dreams coming home rest
beside me, reminders with those white
hot stars long dead even
though their light will not
reach these plains for generations

when I dream
I see it, that eternal solitary fortress
up there on the low sloping hill,
a respite from these days that sting and moan,
from the long lines, the fire-bomb politics,
a home where time stops, space ends

peaceful insignificance

I dream of my father
and of my sister and the long journey
it took to get from my childhood to my grave
and it is there on that hillside where
my final living breath
will be clear
and raw
and free
from smoke and desperation
but also, sadly
from autumn hues and springtime blossoms,
soft silken hair, tears, and love

and when it is time
I will turn the lantern low
step off that wooden porch
and out into that long low
grassland to walk into the darkness
within the dark, the dream eternal
and wake somewhere beyond
starlight, lamplight,
pine and stone and sky

James H Duncan is the editor of *Hobo Camp Review* and the author of *We Are All Terminal But This Exit Is Mine*, *Proper Etiquette in the Slaughterhouse Line*, *Vacancy*, *Beyond the Wounded Horizon*, and other collections of poetry and fiction. He is a former editor with *Writer's Digest*, *American Artist*, and Albany's *Times Union* newspaper, among other publications of varying infamy. When not working on stories, poetry, or novels, he seeks out and reviews independent bookshops for his blog, The Bookshop Hunter.

His lifelong ban from the IHOP on Wurzbach Drive in San Antonio was lifted when they closed in 2015. He currently resides in Albany, New York.

For more, visit www.jameshduncan.com.

Other Works by James Duncan